AN UNPROTECTED FEMALE
AT THE PYRAMIDS
& OTHER STORIES

t2

ANTHONY TROLLOPE

AN UNPROTECTED FEMALE AT THE PYRAMIDS & OTHER STORIES

ALAN SUTTON
1984

Alan Sutton Publishing Limited
17a Brunswick Road
Gloucester GL1 1HG

Copyright © in this edition 1984
Alan Sutton Publishing Limited

British Library Cataloguing in Publication Data

Trollope, Anthony
    An unprotected female at the pyramids.
    I. Title
    823'.8 [F]   PR5681.5

    ISBN 0-86299-129-3

Cover picture: detail from The Pyramids at Gizeh *by
David Roberts
Victoria and Albert Museum, London
Photograph, Bridgeman Art Library.*

Typesetting and origination by
Alan Sutton Publishing Limited
Photoset Bembo 9/10
Printed in Great Britain by
The Guernsey Press Company Limited,
Guernsey, Channel Islands.

CONTENTS

BIOGRAPHICAL NOTE

ANTHONY TROLLOPE (1815–1882), one of the foremost Victorian novelists, is popularly acclaimed for his masterly and genial portraits of a solidly middle class world, dominated by the intrigues of a benevolent landed gentry, with its characteristic settings the parsonage and the hunting field. The familiar Trollope, embodiment of the patrician ideal (in an England whose social fabric was being overturned by pervasive industrial change), has eclipsed the variety of styles and subjects, the tensions and sustained imaginative creations, achieved by a virtuoso literary craftsman whose prolific output included novels of political life, penetrating and memorable character studies, humour, satire, travel books and biography.

Trollope was born on 24 April 1815 in Russell Square, London, and endured a supremely unhappy boyhood, the victim at once of merciless shcoolmasters and school fellows at the great public schools of Harrow, Winchester and again Harrow, of his own gaucheness and of the poverty in which he was raised. His father failed successively in his careers as a barrister, a gentleman farmer and an ecclesiastical historian, reducing the condition of his family from déclassé gentility to one verging on destitution. This was relieved, after an ill-fated trading venture in Ohio, U.S.A., by the timely success of the publication by his mother, Fanny Trollope, of *The Domestic Manners of the Americans* (1832), which immediately established her literary reputation, enabling her thereafter to support the family by her pen.

The family taking refuge from debt in Belgium and Trollope having failed to gain an award to Oxford, he joined the juvenescent General Post Office in 1834 as a clerk. He took little joy in his work until he was transferred in 1841 to the west of Ireland as a postal surveyor. Here he began to enjoy some society and to ride to hounds regularly. He married Rose Heseltine in 1844 and settled in Tipperary. He seized the opportunity to travel the length and breadth of the island on the eve of critical social change. This provided material for his first Irish novels, *The Macdermots of Ballycloran* (1847) and *The Kellys and the O'Kellys* (1848).

Without ceasing to devote himself energetically to his official duties and to regular hunting, by disciplined work he produced a continuous output of novels, culminating in *The Warden* (1855). Excelling in vividly drawn characters, this was acknowledged as his first (but Moderate) success, a scene from clerical life which precedes by two years those of George Eliot. During the next twelve years, he produced a series derived from it which became widely known as the 'Barsetshire' novels (after the imaginary English county in which they are set) and on which his fame most securely rests.

In 1859 Trollope returned to London, resigning from the Civil Service (1867) and standing for Parliament (1868), having 'spawned three books a year'; in total, apart from the Barsetshire series, 18 novels. Outstanding among these are *Orley Farm* (1862), and *Can You Forgive Her?* (1865), the first of the political novels in the voluminous Palliser series which concludes only with *The Duke's Children* (1880).

In 1869 Trollope began his final period as a writer of extended psychological studies based on 'some pathetic incident' (beginning with *He Knew He Was Right)*, problem novels and novels of satire and critisism (such as *The Eustace Diamonds* 1873 and *The Way We Live Now* 1875), mainly published, though not written, serially.

In 1880 Trollope retired from Montagu Square, London, to the Sussex village of Harting as his popularity and his health declined. His later books included a number of travelogues and a biography of *Thackeray* (1879); he was also in demand as an essayist and lecturer. His own candid *Autobiography* (1883) was published posthumously by his son. He died of paralysis in London on 6 December 1882, having written over fifty novels and, by his own estimation, earned some £70,000 by his writing. After his death, his literary reputation suffered a period of neglect, and, condemned for their philistinism, his works one by one went out of print. His position in the history of English fiction, from being a minor cult, is today securely re-established; he is recognised as an entertainer, a versatile stylist and an original and imaginative creator of plots, localities and characters. His parallel career as a civil servant also endures, for he is credited with the invention of the letter-box.

NICHOLAS MANDER

AN UNPROTECTED FEMALE AT THE PYRAMIDS

In the happy days when we were young, no description conveyed to us so complete an idea of mysterious reality as that of an Oriental city. We knew it was actually there, but had such vague notions of its ways and looks! Let any one remember his early impressions as to Bagdad or Grand Cairo, and then say if this was not so. It was probably taken from the 'Arabian Nights,' and the picture produced was one of strange, fantastic, luxurious houses; of women who were either very young and very beautiful, or else very old and very cunning; but in either state exercising much more influence in life than women in the East do now; of good-natured, capricious, though sometimes tyrannical monarchs; and of life full of quaint mysteries, quite unintelligible in every phasis, and on that account the more picturesque.

And perhaps Grand Cairo has thus filled us with more wonder even than Bagdad. We have been in a certain manner at home at Bagdad, but have only visited Grand Cairo occasionally. I know no place which was to me, in early years, so delightfully mysterious as Grand Cairo.

But the route to India and Australia has changed all this. Men from all countries going to the East, now pass through Cairo, and its streets and costumes are no longer strange to us. It has become also a resort for invalids, or rather for those who fear that they may become invalids if they remain in a cold climate during the winter months. And thus at Cairo there is always to be found a considerable population of French, Americans, and of English. Oriental life is brought home to us, dreadfully diluted by western customs, and the delights of the 'Arabian Nights' are shorn of half their value. When we have seen a thing it is never so magnificent to us as when it was half unknown.

It is not much that we deign to learn from these Orientals, – we who glory in our civilization. We do not copy their silence

1

or their abstemiousness, nor that invariable mindfulness of his own personal dignity which always adheres to a Turk or to an Arab. We chatter as much at Cairo as elsewhere, and eat as much and drink as much, and dress ourselves generally in the same old, ugly costume. But we do usually take upon ourselves to wear red caps, and we do ride on donkeys.

Nor are the visitors from the West to Cairo by any means confined to the male sex. Ladies are to be seen in the streets, quite regardless of the Mahommedan custom which presumes a veil to be necessary for an appearance in public; and, to tell the truth, the Mahommedans in general do not appear to be much shocked by their effrontery.

A quarter of the town has in this way become inhabited by men wearing coats and waistcoats, and by women who are without veils; but the English tongue in Egypt finds its centre at Shepheard's Hotel. It is here that people congregate who are looking out for parties to visit with them the Upper Nile, and who are generally all smiles and courtesy; and here also are to be found they who have just returned from this journey, and who are often in a frame of mind towards their companions that is much less amiable. From hence, during the winter, a *cortége* proceeds almost daily to the Pyramids, or to Memphis, or to the petrified forest, or to the City of the Sun. And then, again, four or five times a month the house is filled with young aspirants going out to India, male and female, full of valour and bloom; or with others coming home, no longer young, no longer aspiring, but laden with children and grievances.

The party with whom we are at present concerned is not about to proceed further than the Pyramids, and we shall be able to go with them and return in one and the same day.

It consisted chiefly of an English family, Mr. and Mrs. Damer, their daughter, and two young sons; – of these chiefly, because they were the nucleus to which the others had attached themselves as adherents; they had originated the journey, and in the whole management of it Mr. Damer regarded himself as the master.

The adherents were, firstly, M. Delabordeau, a Frenchman, now resident in Cairo, who had given out that he was in some way concerned in the canal about to be made between the

Mediterranean and the Red Sea. In discussion on this subject he had become acquainted with Mr. Damer; and although the latter gentleman, true to English interests, perpetually declared that the canal would never be made, and thus irritated M. Delabordeau not a little – nevertheless, some measure of friendship had grown up between them.

There was also an American gentleman, Mr. Jefferson Ingram, who was comprising all countries and all nations in one grand tour, as American gentlemen so often do. He was young and good-looking, and had made himself especially agreeable to Mr. Damer, who had declared, more than once, that Mr. Ingram was by far the most rational American he had ever met. Mr. Ingram would listen to Mr. Damer by the half-hour as to the virtue of the British Constitution, and had even sat by almost with patience when Mr. Damer had expressed a doubt as to the good working of the United States' scheme of policy, – which, in an American, was most wonderful. But some of the sojourners at Shepheard's had observed that Mr. Ingram was in the habit of talking with Miss Damer almost as much as with her father, and argued from that, that fond as the young man was of politics, he did sometimes turn his mind to other things also.

And then there was Miss Dawkins. Now Miss Dawkins was an important person, both as to herself and as to her line of life, and she must be described. She was, in the first place, an unprotected female of about thirty years of age. As this is becoming an established profession, setting itself up as it were in opposition to the old-world idea that women, like green peas, cannot come to perfection without supporting-sticks, it will be understood at once what were Miss Dawkins' sentiments. She considered – or at any rate so expressed herself – that peas could grow very well without sticks, and could not only grow thus unsupported, but could also make their way about the world without any incumbrance of sticks whatsoever. She did not intend, she said, to rival Ida Pfeiffer, seeing that she was attached in a moderate way to bed and board, and was attached to society in a manner almost more than moderate; but she had no idea of being prevented from seeing anything she wished to see because she had neither father, nor husband, nor brother available for the purpose of escort. She was a human creature, with arms and legs, she said; and she intended to use them. And this was all very well; but nevertheless she had a strong inclination to use the arms and legs of other people when she could make them serviceable.

In person Miss Dawkins was not without attraction. I should exaggerate if I were to say that she was beautiful and elegant; but she was good looking, and not usually ill mannered. She was tall, and gifted with features rather sharp and with eyes very bright. Her hair was of the darkest shade of brown, and was always worn in *bandeaux*, very neatly. She appeared generally in black, though other circumstances did not lead one to suppose that she was in mourning; and then, no other travelling costume is so convenient! She always wore a dark broad-brimmed straw hat, as to the ribbons on which she was rather particular. She was very neat about her gloves and boots; and though it cannot be said that her dress was got up without reference to expense, there can be no doubt that it was not effected without considerable outlay, – and more considerable thought.

Miss Dawkins – Sabrina Dawkins was her name, but she seldom had friends about her intimate enough to use the word Sabrina, – was certainly a clever young woman. She could talk on most subjects, if not well, at least well enough to amuse. If she had not read much, she never showed any lamentable deficiency; she was good-humoured, as a rule, and could on occasions be very soft and winning. People who had known her long would sometimes say that she was selfish; but with new acquaintance she was forbearing and self-denying.

With what income Miss Dawkins was blessed no one seemed to know. She lived like a gentlewoman, as far as outward appearance went, and never seemed to be in want; but some people would say that she knew very well how many sides there were to a shilling, and some enemy had once declared that she was an 'old soldier.' Such was Miss Dawkins.

She also, as well as Mr. Ingram and M. Delabordeau, had laid herself out to find the weak side of Mr. Damer. Mr. Damer, with all his family, was going up the Nile, and it was known that he had room for two in his boat over and above his own family. Miss Dawkins had told him that she had not quite made up her mind to undergo so great a fatigue, but that, nevertheless, she had a longing of the soul to see something of Nubia. To this Mr. Damer had answered nothing but 'Oh!' which Miss Dawkins had not found to be encouraging.

But she had not on that account despaired. To a married man there are always two sides, and in this instance there was Mrs. Damer as well as Mr. Damer. When Mr. Damer said 'Oh!' Miss Dawkins sighed, and said, 'Yes, indeed!' then smiled, and betook herself to Mrs. Damer.

Now Mrs. Damer was soft-hearted, and also somewhat old-fashioned. She did not conceive any violent affection for Miss Dawkins, but she told her daughter that 'the single lady by herself was a very nice young woman, and that it was a thousand pities she should have to go about so much alone like.'

Miss Damer had turned up her pretty nose, thinking, perhaps, how small was the chance that it ever should be her own lot to be an unprotected female. But Miss Dawkins carried her point at any rate as regarded the expedition to the Pyramids.

Miss Damer, I have said, had a pretty nose. I may also say that she had pretty eyes, mouth, and chin, with other necessary appendages, all pretty. As to the two Master Damers, who were respectively of the ages of fifteen and sixteen, it may be sufficient to say that they were conspicuous for red caps and for the constancy with which they raced their donkeys.

And now the donkeys, and the donkey-boys, and the dragomans were all standing at the steps of Shepheard's Hotel. To each donkey there was a donkey-boy, and to each gentleman there was a dragoman, so that a goodly *cortége* was assembled, and a goodly noise was made. It may here be remarked, perhaps with some little pride, that not half the noise is given in Egypt to persons speaking any other language that is bestowed on those whose vocabulary is English.

This lasted for half an hour. Had the party been French the donkeys would have arrived only fifteen minutes before the appointed time. And then out came Damer père and Damer

mère, Damer fille and Damer fils. Damer mère was leaning on
her husband, as was her wont. She was not an unprotected
female, and had no desire to make any attempts in that line.
Damer fille was attended sedulously by Mr. Ingram, for
whose demolishment, however, Mr. Damer still brought up,
in a loud voice, the fag ends of certain political arguments
which he would fain have poured direct into the ears of his
opponent, had not his wife been so persistent in claiming her
privileges. M. Delabordeau should have followed with Miss
Dawkins, but his French politeness, or else his fear of the
unprotected female, taught him to walk on the other side of
the mistress of the party.

Miss Dawkins left the house with an eager young Damer
yelling on each side of her; but nevertheless, though thus
neglected by the gentlemen of the party, she was all smiles and
prettiness, and looked so sweetly on Mr. Ingram when that
gentleman stayed a moment to help her on to her donkey, that
his heart almost misgave him for leaving her as soon as she
was in her seat.

And then they were off. In going from the hotel to the
Pyramids our party had not to pass through any of the queer
old narrow streets of the true Cairo – Cairo the Oriental.
They all lay behind them as they went down by the back of
the hotel, by the barracks of the Pasha and the College of the
Dervishes, to the village of old Cairo and the banks of the
Nile.

Here they were kept half an hour while their dragomans
made a bargain with the ferryman, a stately reis, or captain of
the boat, who declared with much dignity that he could not
carry them over for a sum less than six times the amount to
which he was justly entitled; when the dragomans, with great
energy on behalf of their masters, offered him only five times
that sum. As far as the reis was concerned, the contest might
soon have been at an end, for the man was not without a
conscience; and would have been content with five times and a
half; but then the three dragomans quarrelled among themselves as to which should have the paying of the money, and the
affair became very tedious.

'What horrid, odious men!' said Miss Dawkins, appealing
to Mr. Damer. 'Do you think they will let us go over at all?'

'Well, I suppose they will; people do get over generally, I believe. Abdallah! Abdallah! why don't you pay the man? That fellow is always striving to save half a piastre for me.'

'I wish he wasn't quite so particular,' said Mrs. Damer, who was already becoming rather tired; 'but I'm sure he's a very honest man in trying to protect us from being robbed.'

'That he is,' said Miss Dawkins. 'What a delightful trait of national character it is to see these men so faithful to their employers!' And then at last they got over the ferry, Mr. Ingram having descended among the combatants, and settled the matter in dispute by threats and shouts, and an uplifted stick.

They crossed the broad Nile exactly at the spot where the nilometer, or river gauge, measures from day to day, and from year to year, the increasing or decreasing treasures of the stream, and landed at a village where thousands of eggs are made into chickens by the process of artificial incubation.

Mrs. Damer thought that it was very hard upon the maternal hens – the hens which should have been maternal – that they should be thus robbed of the delights of motherhood.

'So unnatural, you know,' said Miss Dawkins; 'so opposed to the fostering principles of creation. Don't you think so, Mr. Ingram?'

Mr. Ingram said he didn't know. He was again seating Miss Damer on her donkey, and it must be presumed that he performed this feat clumsily; for Fanny Damer could jump on and off the animal with hardly a finger to help her, when her brother or her father was her escort; but now, under the hands of Mr. Ingram, this work of mounting was one which required considerable time and care. All which Miss Dawkins observed with precision.

'It's all very well talking,' said Mr. Damer, bringing up his donkey nearly alongside of that of Mr. Ingram, and ignoring his daughter's presence, just as he would have done that of his dog; 'but you must admit that political power is more equally distributed in England than it is in America.'

'Perhaps it is,' said Mr. Ingram; 'equally distributed among, we will say, three dozen families,' and he made a feint as though to hold in his impetuous donkey, using the spur,

however, at the same time on the side that was unseen by Mr.
Damer. As he did so, Fanny's donkey became equally impetuous, and the two cantered on in advance of the whole party.
It was quite in vain that Mr. Damer, at the top of his voice,
shouted out something about 'three dozen corruptible dema-
gogues.' Mr. Ingram found it quite impossible to restrain his
donkey so as to listen to the sarcasm.

'I do believe papa would talk politics,' said Fanny, 'if he
were at the top of Mont Blanc, or under the Falls of Niagara. I
do hate politics, Mr. Ingram.'

'I am sorry for that, very,' said Mr. Ingram, almost sadly.

'Sorry, why? You don't want me to talk politics, do you?'

'In America we are all politicians, more or less; and,
therefore, I suppose you will hate us all.'

'Well, I rather think I should,' said Fanny; 'you would be
such bores.' But there was something in her eye, as she spoke,
which atoned for the harshness of her words.

'A very nice young man is Mr. Ingram; don't you think
so?' said Miss Dawkins to Mrs. Damer. Mrs. Damer was
going along upon her donkey, not altogether comfortably.
She much wished to have her lord and legitimate protector
by her side, but he had left her to the care of a dragoman
whose English was not intelligible to her, and she was rather
cross.

'Indeed, Miss Dawkins, I don't know who are nice and who
are not. This nasty donkey stumbles at every step. There! I
know I shall be down directly.'

'You need not be at all afraid of that; they are perfectly safe,
I believe, always,' said Miss Dawkins rising in her stirrup, and
handling her reins quite triumphantly. 'A very little practice
will make you quite at home.'

'I don't know what you mean by a very little practice. I
have been here six weeks. Why did you put me on such a bad
donkey as this?' and she turned to Abdallah, the dragoman.

'Him berry good donkey, my lady; berry good, – best of
all. Call him Jack in Cairo. Him go to Pyramid and back, and
mind noting.'

'What does he say, Miss Dawkins?'

'He says that that donkey is one called Jack. If so I've had
him myself many times, and Jack is a very good donkey.'

'I wish you had him now with all my heart,' said Mrs.
Damer. Upon which Miss Dawkins offered to change; but
those perils of mounting and dismounting were to Mrs.
Damer a great deal too severe to admit of this.

'Seven miles of canal to be carried out into the sea, at a
minimum depth of twenty-three feet, and the stone to be
fetched from Heaven knows where! All the money in France
wouldn't do it.' This was addressed by Mr. Damer to M.
Delabordeau, whom he had caught after the abrupt flight of
Mr. Ingram.

'Den we will borrow a leetle from England,' said M.
Delabordeau.

'Precious little, I can tell you. Such stock would not hold its
price in our markets for twenty-four hours. If it were made,
the freights would be too heavy to allow of merchandise
passing through. The heavy goods would all go round; and as
for passengers and mails, you don't expect to get them, I
suppose, while there is a railroad ready made to their hand?'

'Ve vill carry all your ships through vidout any transporta-
tion. Think of that, my friend.'

'Pshaw! You are worse than Ingram. Of all the plans I ever
heard of it is the most monstrous, the most impracticable, the
most –' But here he was interrupted by the entreaties of his
wife, who had, in absolute deed and fact, slipped from her
donkey, and was now calling lustily for her husband's aid.
Whereupon Miss Dawkins allied herself to the Frenchman,
and listened with an air of strong conviction to those arguments which were so weak in the ears of Mr. Damer. M.
Delabordeau was about to ride across the Great Desert to
Jerusalem, and it might perhaps be quite as well to do that
with him, as to go up the Nile as far as the second cataract
with the Damers.

'And so, M. Delabordeau, you intend really to start for
Mount Sinai?'

'Yes mees; ve intend to make one start on Monday week.'

'And so on to Jerusalem. You are quite right. It would be a
thousand pities to be in these countries, and to return without
going over such ground as that. I shall certainly go to
Jerusalem myself by that route.'

'Vot mees! you? Vould you not find it too much fatigante?'

'I care nothing for fatigue, if I like the party I am with, –
nothing at all, literally. You will hardly understand me,
perhaps, M. Delabordeau; but I do not see any reason why I,
as a young woman, should not make any journey that is
practicable for a young man.'

'Ah! dat is great resolution for you, mees.'

'I mean as far as fatigue is concerned. You are a Frenchman,
and belong to the nation that is at the head of all human
civilization –'

M. Delabordeau took off his hat and bowed low, to the
peak of his donkey saddle. He dearly loved to hear his country
praised, as Miss Dawkins was aware.

'And I am sure you must agree with me,' continued Miss
Dawkins, 'that the time is gone by for women to consider
themselves helpless animals, or to be so considered by others.'

'Mees Dawkins vould never be considered, not in any times
at all, to be one helpless animal,' said M. Delabordeau, civilly.

'I do not, at any rate, intend to be so regarded,' said she. 'It
suits me to travel alone; not that I am averse to society; quite
the contrary; if I meet pleasant people I am always ready to
join them. But it suits me to travel without any permanent
party, and I do not see why false shame should prevent my
seeing the world as thoroughly as though I belonged to the
other sex. Why should it, M. Delabordeau?'

M. Delabordeau declared that he did not see any reason
why it should.

'I am passionately anxious to stand upon Mount Sinai,'
continued Miss Dawkins; 'to press with my feet the earliest
spot in sacred history, of the identity of which we are certain;
to feel within me the awe-inspiring thrill of that thrice sacred
hour!'

The Frenchman looked as though he did not quite understand her, but he said that it would be magnifique.

'You have already made up your party, I suppose, M.
Delabordeau?'

M. Delabordeau gave the names of two Frenchmen and one
Englishman who were going with him.

'Upon my word it is a great temptation to join you,' said
Miss Dawkins, 'only for that horrid Englishman.'

'Vat, Mr. Stanley?'

'Oh, I don't mean any disrespect to Mr. Stanley. The horridness I speak of does not attach to him personally, but to his stiff, respectable, ungainly, well-behaved, irrational, and uncivilised country. You see I am not very patriotic.'

'Not quite so much as my dear friend Mr. Damer.'

'Ha! ha! ha! an excellent creature, isn't he? And so they all are; dear creatures. But then they are so backward. They are most anxious that I should join them up the Nile, but – ,' and then Miss Dawkins shrugged her shoulders gracefully, and, as she flattered herself, like a Frenchwoman. After that they rode on in silence for a few moments.

'Yes, I must see Mount Sinai,' said Miss Dawkins, and then sighed deeply. M. Delabordeau, notwithstanding that his country does stand at the head of all human civilization, was not courteous enough to declare that if Miss Dawkins would join his party across the desert, nothing would be wanting to make his beatitude in this world perfect.

Their road from the village of the chicken-hatching ovens lay up along the left bank of the Nile, through an immense grove of lofty palm-trees, looking out from among which our visitors could ever and anon see the heads of the two great pyramids; – that is, such of them could see it as felt any solicitude in the matter.

It is astonishing how such things lose their great charm as men find themselves in their close neighbourhood. To one living in New York or London, how ecstatic is the interest inspired by these huge structures. One feels that no price would be too high to pay for seeing them as long as time and distance, and the world's inexorable task-work forbid such a visit. How intense would be the delight of climbing over the wondrous handiwork of those wondrous architects so long since dead; how thrilling the awe with which one would penetrate down into their interior caves – those caves in which lay buried the bones of ancient kings, whose very names seem to have come to us almost from another world!

But all these feelings become strangely dim, their acute edges wonderfully worn, as the subjects which inspired them are brought near to us. 'Ah! so those are the Pyramids, are they?' says the traveller, when the first glimpse of them is shown to him from the window of a railway carriage. 'Dear me; they don't look so very high, do they? For Heaven's sake put the blind down, or we shall be destroyed by the dust.' And then the ecstacy and keen delight of the Pyramids has vanished, and for ever.

Our friends, therefore, who for weeks past had seen them from a distance, though they had not yet visited them, did not seem to have any strong feeling on the subject as they trotted through the grove of palm-trees. Mr. Damer had not yet escaped from his wife, who was still fretful from the result of her little accident.

'It was all the chattering of that Miss Dawkins,' said Mrs. Damer. 'She would not let me attend to what I was doing.'

'Miss Dawkins is an ass,' said her husband.

'It is a pity she has no one to look after her,' said Mrs. Damer.

M. Delabordeau was still listening to Miss Dawkins's raptures about Mount Sinai. 'I wonder whether she has got any money,' said M. Delabordeau to himself. 'It can't be much,' he went on thinking, 'or she would not be left in this way by herself.' And the result of his thoughts was that Miss Dawkins, if undertaken, might probably become more plague than profit. As to Miss Dawkins herself, though she was ecstatic about Mount Sinai – which was not present – she seemed to have forgotten the poor Pyramids, which were then before her nose.

The two lads were riding races along the dusty path much to the disgust of their donkey-boys. Their time for enjoyment was to come. There were hampers to be opened; and then the absolute climbing of the Pyramids would actually be a delight to them.

As for Miss Damer and Mr. Ingram, it was clear that they had forgotten palm-trees, Pyramids, the Nile, and all Egypt. They had escaped to a much fairer paradise.

'Could I bear to live among Republicans?' said Fanny, repeating the last words of her American lover, and looking down from her donkey to the ground as she did so. 'I hardly know what Republicans are, Mr. Ingram.'

'Let me teach you,' said he.

'You do talk such nonsense. I declare there is that Miss Dawkins looking at us as though she had twenty eyes. Could you not teach her, Mr. Ingram?'

And so they emerged from the palm-tree grove, through a village crowded with dirty, straggling Arab children, on to the cultivated plain, beyond which the Pyramids stood, now full before them; the two large Pyramids, a smaller one, and the huge sphinx's head all in a group together.

'Fanny,' said Bob Damer, riding up to her, 'mamma wants you; so toddle back.'

'Mamma wants me! What can she want me for now?' said Fanny, with a look of anything but filial duty in her face.

'To protect her from Miss Dawkins, I think. She wants you to ride at her side, so that Dawkins mayn't get at her. Now, Mr. Ingram, I'll bet you half a crown I'm at the top of the big Pyramid before you.'

Poor Fanny! She obeyed, however; doubtless feeling that it would not do as yet to show too plainly that she preferred Mr. Ingram to her mother. She arrested her donkey, therefore, till Mrs. Damer overtook her; and Mr. Ingram, as he paused for a moment with her while she did so, fell into the hands of Miss Dawkins.

'I cannot think, Fanny, how you get on so quick,' said Mrs. Damer. 'I'm always last; but then my donkey is such a very nasty one. Look there, now; he's always trying to get me off.'

'We shall soon be at the Pyramids now, mamma.'

'How on earth I am ever to get back again I cannot think. I am so tired now that I can hardly sit.'

'You'll be better, mamma, when you get your luncheon and a glass of wine.'

'How on earth we are to eat and drink with those nasty Arab people around us, I can't conceive. They tell me we shall be eaten up by them. But, Fanny, what has Mr. Ingram been saying to you all the day?'

'What has he been saying, mamma? Oh! I don't know; – a hundred things, I dare say. But he has not been talking to me all the time.'

'I think he has, Fanny, nearly, since we crossed the river. Oh, dear! oh, dear! this animal does hurt me so! Every time he moves he flings his head about, and that gives me such a bump.' And then Fanny commiserated her mother's sufferings, and in her commiseration contrived to elude any further questionings as to Mr. Ingram's conversation.

'Majestic piles, are they not?' said Miss Dawkins, who, having changed her companion, allowed her mind to revert from Mount Sinai to the Pyramids. They were now riding through cultivated ground, with the vast extent of the sands of Libya before them. The two Pyramids were standing on the margin of the sand, with the head of the recumbent sphynx plainly visible between them. But no idea can be formed of the size of this immense figure till it is visited much more closely. The body is covered with sand, and the head and neck alone stand above the surface of the ground. They were still two miles distant, and the sphynx as yet was but an obscure mound between the two vast Pyramids.

'Immense piles!' said Miss Dawkins, repeating her own words.

'Yes, they are large,' said Mr. Ingram, who did not choose to indulge in enthusiasm in the presence of Miss Dawkins.

'Enormous! What a grand idea! – eh, Mr. Ingram? The human race does not create such things as those nowadays!'

'No, indeed,' he answered; 'but perhaps we create better things.'

'Better! You do not mean to say, Mr. Ingram, that you are an utilitarian. I do, in truth, hope better things of you than that. Yes! steam mills are better, no doubt, and mechanics' institutes, and penny newspapers. But is nothing to be valued but what is useful?' And Miss Dawkins, in the height of her enthusiasm, switched her donkey severely over the shoulder.

'I might, perhaps, have said also that we create more beautiful things,' said Mr. Ingram.

'But we cannot create older things.'

'No, certainly; we cannot do that.'

'Nor can we imbue what we do create with the grand associations which environ those piles with so intense an interest. Think of the mighty dead, Mr. Ingram, and of their great homes when living. Think of the hands which it took to raise those huge blocks –'

'And of the lives which it cost.'

'Doubtless. The tyranny and invincible power of the royal architects add to the grandeur of the idea. One would not wish to have back the kings of Egypt.'

'Well, no; they would be neither useful nor beautiful.'

'Perhaps not; and I do not wish to be picturesque at the expense of my fellow-creatures.'

'I doubt, even, whether they would be picturesque.'

'You know what I mean, Mr. Ingram. But the associations of such names, and the presence of the stupendous works with which they are connected, fill the soul with awe. Such, at least, is the effect with mine.'

'I fear that my tendencies, Miss Dawkins, are more realistic than your own.'

'You belong to a young country, Mr. Ingram, and are naturally prone to think of material life. The necessity of living looms large before you.'

'Very large, indeed, Miss Dawkins.'

'Whereas with us, with some of us at least, the material aspect has given place to one in which poetry and enthusiasm prevail. To such among us the associations of past times are very dear. Cheops, to me, is more than Napoleon Bonaparte.'

'That is more than most of your countrymen can say, at any rate, just at present.'

'I am a woman,' continued Miss Dawkins.

Mr. Ingram took off his hat in acknowledgment both of the announcement and of the fact.

'And to us it is not given – not given as yet – to share in the great deeds of the present. The envy of your sex has driven us from the paths which lead to honour. But the deeds of the past are as much ours as yours.'

'Oh, quite as much.'

''Tis to your country that we look for enfranchisement from this thraldom. Yes, Mr. Ingram, the women of America have that strength of mind which has been wanting to those of Europe. In the United States woman will at last learn to exercise her proper mission.'

Mr. Ingram expressed a sincere wish that such might be the case; and then wondering at the ingenuity with which Miss Dawkins had travelled round from Cheops and his Pyramid to the rights of women in America, he contrived to fall back, under the pretence of asking after the ailments of Mrs. Damer.

And now at last they were on the sand, in the absolute desert, making their way up to the very foot of the most northern of the two Pyramids. They were by this time

surrounded by a crowd of Arab guides, or Arabs professing to
be guides, who had already ascertained that Mr. Damer was
the chief of the party, and were accordingly driving him
almost to madness by the offers of their services, and their
assurance that he could not possibly see the outside or the
inside of either structure, or even remain alive upon the
ground, unless he at once accepted their offers made at their
own prices.

'Get away, will you?' said he. 'I don't want any of you, and I
won't have you! If you take hold of me I'll shoot you!' This
was said to one specially energetic Arab, who, in his efforts to
secure his prey, had caught hold of Mr. Damer by the leg.

'Yes, yes, I say! Englishmen always take me; – me – me, and
then no break him leg. Yes – yes – yes; – I go. Master say, yes.
Only one leetle ten shilling!'

'Abdallah!' shouted Mr. Damer, 'why don't you take this
man away? Why don't you make him understand that if all the
Pyramids depended on it, I would not give him sixpence!'

And then Abdallah, thus invoked, came up, and explained
to the man in Arabic that he would gain his object more surely
if he would behave himself a little more quietly; a hint which
the man took for one minute, and for one minute only.

And then poor Mrs. Damer replied to an application for
backsheish by the gift of a sixpence. Unfortunate woman! The
word backsheish means, I believe, a gift; but it has come in
Egypt to signify money, and is eternally dinned into the ears
of strangers by Arab suppliants. Mrs. Damer ought to have
known better, as, during the last six weeks she had never
shown her face out of Shepheard's Hotel without being
pestered for backsheish; but she was tired and weak, and
foolishly thought to rid herself of the man who was annoying
her.

No sooner had the coin dropped from her hand into that of
the Arab, than she was surrounded by a cluster of beggars,
who loudly made their petitions as though they would, each
of them, individually be injured if treated with less liberality
than the first comer. They took hold of her donkey, her
bridle, her saddle, her legs and at last her arms and hands,
screaming for backsheish in voices that were neither sweet nor
mild.

In her dismay she did give away sundry small coins — all, probably, that she had about her; but this only made the matter worse. Money was going, and each man, by sufficient energy, might hope to get some of it. They were very energetic, and so frightened the poor lady that she would certainly have fallen, had she not been kept on her seat by their pressure around her.

'Oh, dear! oh, dear! get away,' she cried. 'I haven't got any more; indeed, I haven't. Go away, I tell you! Mr. Damer! oh, Mr. Damer!' and then, in the excess of her agony, she uttered one loud, long, and continuous shriek.

Up came Mr. Damer; up came Abdallah; up came M. Delabordeau; up came Mr. Ingram, and at last she was rescued. 'You shouldn't go away, and leave me to the mercy of these nasty people. As to that Abdallah, he is of no use to anybody.'

'Why you bodder de good lady, you dem blackguard?' said Abdallah, raising his stick, as though he were going to lay them all low with a blow. 'Now you get noting, you tief!'

The Arabs for a moment retired to a little distance, like flies driven from a sugar-bowl; but it was easy to see that, like the flies, they would return at the first vacant moment.

And now they had reached the very foot of the Pyramids and proceeded to dismount from their donkeys. Their intention was first to ascend to the top, then to come down to their banquet, and after that to penetrate into the interior. And all this would seem to be easy of performace. The Pyramid is undoubtedly high, but it is so constructed as to admit of climbing without difficulty. A lady mounting it would undoubtedly need some assistance, but any man possessed of moderate activity would require no aid at all.

But our friends were at once imbued with the tremendous nature of the task before them. A sheikh of the Arabs came forth, who communicated with them through Abdallah. The work could be done, no doubt, he said; but a great many men would be wanted to assist. Each lady must have four Arabs, and each gentleman three; and then, seeing that the work would be peculiarly severe on this special day, each of these numerous Arabs must be remunerated by some very large number of piastres.

Mr. Damer, who was by no means a close man in his money dealings, opened his eyes with surprise, and mildly expostulated; M. Delabordeau, who was rather a close man in his reckonings, immediately buttoned up his breeches-pocket and declared that he should decline to mount the Pyramid at all at that price; and then Mr. Ingram descended to the combat.

The protestations of the men were fearful. They declared, with loud voices, eager actions, and manifold English oaths, that an attempt was being made to rob them. They had a right to demand the sums which they were charging, and it was a shame that English gentlemen should come and take the bread out of their mouths. And so they screeched, gesticulated, and swore, and frightened poor Mrs. Damer almost into fits.

But at last it was settled and away they started, the sheikh declaring that the bargain had been made at so low a rate as to leave him not one piastre for himself. Each man had an Arab on each side of him, and Miss Dawkins and Miss Damer had each, in addition, one behind. Mrs. Damer was so frightened as altogether to have lost all ambition to ascend. She sat below on a fragment of stone, with the three dragomans standing around her as guards; but even with the three dragomans the attacks on her were so frequent, and as she declared afterwards she was so bewildered, that she never had time to remember that she had come there from England to see the Pyramids, and that she was now immediately under them.

The boys, utterly ignoring their guides, scrambled up quicker than the Arabs could follow them. Mr. Damer started off at a pace which soon brought him to the end of his tether, and from that point was dragged up by the sheer strength of his assistants; thereby accomplishing the wishes of the men, who induce their victims to start as rapidly as possible, in order that they may soon find themselves helpless from want of wind. Mr. Ingram endeavoured to attach himself to Fanny, and she would have been nothing loth to have him at her right hand instead of the hideous brown, shrieking, one-eyed Arab who took hold of her. But it was soon found that any such arrangement was impossible. Each guide felt that if he lost his own peculiar hold he would lose his prey, and held on, therefore, with invincible tenacity. Miss Dawkins looked, too, as though she had thought to be attended to by some Christian cavalier, but no Christian cavalier was forthcoming. M. Delabordeau was the wisest, for he took the matter quietly, did as he was bid, and allowed the guides nearly to carry him to the top of the edifice.

'Ha! So this is the top of the Pyramid, is it?' said Mr. Damer, bringing out his words one by one, being terribly out of breath. 'Very wonderful, very wonderful indeed!'

'It is wonderful,' said Miss Dawkins, whose breath had not failed her in the least, 'very wonderful indeed. Only think, Mr. Damer, you might travel on for days and days, till days became months, through those interminable sands, and yet you would never come to the end of them. Is it not quite stupendous?'

'Ah, yes, quite, – puff, puff' – said Mr. Damer, striving to regain his breath.

Mr. Damer was now at her disposal; weak and worn with toil and travel, out of breath, and with half his manhood gone; if ever she might prevail over him so as to procure from his mouth an assent to that Nile proposition, it would be now. And after all, that Nile proposition was the best one now before her. She did not quite like the idea of starting off across the Great Desert without any lady, and was not sure that she was prepared to be fallen in love with by M. Delabordeau, even if there should ultimately be any readiness on the part of that gentleman to perform the rôle of lover. With Mr. Ingram the matter was different, nor was she so diffident of her own charms as to think it altogether impossible that she might succeed, in the teeth of that little chit, Fanny Damer. That Mr. Ingram would join the party up the Nile she had very little doubt; and then there would be one place left for her. She would thus, at any rate, become commingled with a most respectable family, who might be of material service to her.

Thus actuated she commenced an earnest attack upon Mr. Damer.

'Stupendous!' she said again, for she was fond of repeating favourite words. 'What a wondrous race must have been those Egyptian kings of old!'

'I dare say they were,' said Mr. Damer, wiping his brow as he sat upon a large loose stone, a fragment lying on the flat top of the Pyramid, one of those stones with which the complete apex was once made, or was once about to be made.

'A magnificent race! so gigantic in their conceptions! Their ideas altogether overwhelm us poor, insignificant, latter-day mortals. They built these vast Pyramids; but for us, it is task enough to climb to their top.'

'Quite enough,' ejaculated Mr. Damer.

But Mr. Damer would not always remain weak and out of breath, and it was absolutely necessary for Miss Dawkins to hurry away from Cheops and his tomb, to Thebes and Karnac.

'After seeing this it is impossible for any one with a spark of imagination to leave Egypt without going further a-field.'

Mr. Damer merely wiped his brow and grunted. This Miss Dawkins took as a signal of weakness, and went on with her task perseveringly.

'For myself, I have resolved to go up, at any rate as far as Asouan and the first cataract. I had thought of acceding to the wishes of a party who are going across the Great Desert by Mount Sinai to Jerusalem; but the kindness of yourself and Mrs. Damer is so great, and the prospect of joining in your boat is so pleasurable, that I have made up my mind to accept your very kind offer.'

This, it will be acknowledged, was bold on the part of Miss Dawkins; but what will not audacity effect? To use the slang of modern language, cheek carries everything nowadays. And whatever may have been Miss Dawkins's deficiencies, in this virtue she was not deficient.

'I have made up my mind to accept your very kind offer,' she said, shining on Mr. Damer with her blandest smile.

What was a stout, breathless, perspiring, middle-aged gentleman to do under such circumstances? Mr. Damer was a man who, in most matters, had his own way. That his wife should have given such an invitation without consulting him, was, he knew, quite impossible. She would as soon have thought of asking all those Arab guides to accompany them. Nor was it to be thought of that he should allow himself to be kidnapped into such an arrangement by the impudence of any Miss Dawkins. But there was, he felt, a difficulty in answering such a proposition from a young lady with a direct negative, especially while he was so scant of breath. So he wiped his brow again, and looked at her.

'But I can only agree to this on one understanding,' continued Miss Dawkins, 'and that is, that I am allowed to defray my own full share of the expense of the journey.'

Upon hearing this Mr. Damer thought that he saw his way out of the wood. 'Wherever I go, Miss Dawkins, I am always the paymaster myself,' and this he contrived to say with some sternness, palpitating though he still was; and the sternness which was deficient in his voice he endeavoured to put into his countenance.

But he did not know Miss Dawkins. 'Oh, Mr. Damer,' she said, and as she spoke her smile became almost blander than it was before; 'oh, Mr. Damer, I could not think of suffering you to be so liberal; I could not, indeed. But I shall be quite content that you should pay everything, and let me settle with you in one sum afterwards.'

Mr. Damer's breath was now rather more under his own command. 'I am afraid, Miss Dawkins,' he said, 'that Mrs. Damer's weak state of health will not admit of such an arrangement.'

'What, about the paying?'

'Not only as to that, but we are a family party, Miss Dawkins; and great as would be the benefit of your society to all of us, in Mrs. Damer's present state of health, I am afraid – in short, you would not find it agreeable. – And therefore –' this he added, seeing that she was still about to persevere – 'I fear that we must forego the advantage you offer.'

And then, looking into his face, Miss Dawkins did perceive that even her audacity would not prevail.

'Oh, very well,' she said, and moving from the stone on which she had been sitting, she walked off, carrying her head very high, to a corner of the Pyramid from which she could look forth alone towards the sands of Libya.

In the mean time another little overture was being made on the top of the same pyramid, – an overture which was not received quite in the same spirit. While Mr. Damer was recovering his breath for the sake of answering Miss Dawkins, Miss Damer had walked to the further corner of the square platform on which they were placed, and there sat herself

down with her face turned towards Cairo. Perhaps it was not
singular that Mr. Ingram should have followed her.

This would have been very well if a dozen Arabs had not
also followed them. But as this was the case, Mr. Ingram had
to play his game under some difficulty. He had no sooner
seated himself beside her than they came and stood directly in
front of the seat, shutting out the view, and by no means
improving the fragrance of the air around them.

'And this then, Miss Damer, will be our last excursion
together,' he said, in his tenderest, softest tone.

'De good Englishman will gib de poor Arab one little
backsheish,' said an Arab, putting out his hand and shaking
Mr. Ingrams's shoulder.

'Yes, yes, yes; him gib backsheish,' said another.

'Him berry good man,' said a third, putting up his filthy
hand, and touching Mr. Ingram's face.

'And young lady berry good, too; she give backsheish to
poor Arab.'

'Yes,' said a fourth, preparing to take a similar liberty with
Miss Damer.

This was too much for Mr. Ingram. He had already used
very positive language in his endeavour to assure his tormen-
tors that they would not get a piastre from him. But this only
changed their soft persuasions into threats. Upon hearing
which, and upon seeing what the man attempted to do in his
endeavour to get money from Miss Damer, he raised his stick,
and struck first one and then the other as violently as he could
upon their heads.

Any ordinary civilized men would have been stunned by
such blows, for they fell on the bare foreheads of the Arabs;
but the objects of the American's wrath merely skulked away;
and the others, convinced by the only arguments which they
understood, followed in pursuit of victims who might be less
pugnacious.

It is hard for a man to be at once tender and pugnacious – to
be sentimental, while he is putting forth his physical strength
with all the violence in his power. It is difficult, also, for him
to be gentle instantly after having been in a rage. So he
changed his tactics at the moment, and came to the point at
once in a manner befitting his present state of mind.

'Those vile wretches have put me in such a heat,' he said, 'that I hardly know what I am saying. But the fact is this, Miss Damer, I cannot leave Cairo without knowing –. You understand what I mean, Miss Damer.'

'Indeed I do not, Mr. Ingram; except that I am afraid you mean nonsense.'

'Yes, you do; you know that I love you. I am sure you must know it. At any rate you know it now.'

'Mr. Ingram, you should not talk in such a way.'

'Why should I not? But the truth is, Fanny, I can talk in no other way. I do love you dearly. Can you love me well enough to go and be my wife in a country far away from your own?'

Before she left the top of the Pyramid Fanny Damer had said that she would try.

Mr. Ingram was now a proud and happy man, and seemed to think the steps of the Pyramid too small for his elastic energy. But Fanny feared that her troubles were to come. There was papa – that terrible bugbear on all such occasions. What would papa say? She was sure her papa would not allow her to marry and go so far away from her own family and country. For herself, she liked the Americans – always had liked them; so she said; – would desire nothing better than to live among them. But papa! And Fanny sighed as she felt that all the recognized miseries of a young lady in love were about to fall upon her.

Nevertheless, at her lover's instance, she promised, and declared, in twenty different loving phrases, that nothing on earth should ever make her false to her love or to her lover.

'Fanny, where are you? Why are you not ready to come down?' shouted Mr. Damer, not in the best of tempers. He felt that he had almost been unkind to an unprotected female, and his heart misgave him. And yet it would have misgiven him more had he allowed himself to be entrapped by Miss Dawkins.

'I am quite ready, papa,' said Fanny, running up to him – for it may be understood that there is quite room enough for a young lady to run on the top of the Pyramid.

'I am sure I don't know where you have been all the time,' said Mr. Damer; 'and where are those two boys?'

Fanny pointed to the top of the other Pyramid, and there they were, conspicuous with their red caps.

'And M. Delabordeau?'

'Oh! he has gone down, I think; – no, he is there with Miss Dawkins.' And in truth Mis Dawkins was leaning on his arm most affectionately, as she stooped over and looked down upon the ruins below her.

'And where is that fellow, Ingram?' said Mr. Damer, looking about him 'He is always out of the way when he's wanted.'

To this Fanny said nothing. Why should she? She was not Mr. Ingram's keeper.

And then they all descended, each again with his proper number of Arabs to hurry and embarrass him; and they found Mrs. Damer at the bottom, like a piece of sugar covered with flies. She was heard to declare afterwards that she would not go to the Pyramids again, not if they were to be given to her for herself, as ornaments for her garden.

The picnic lunch among the big stones at the foot of the Pyramid was not a very gay affair. Miss Dawkins talked more than any one else, being determined to show that she bore her defeat gallantly. Her conversation, however, was chiefly addressed to M. Delabordeau, and he seemed to think more of his cold chicken and ham than he did of her wit and attention.

Fanny hardly spoke a word. There was her father before her, and she could not eat, much less talk, as she thought of all that she would have to go through. What would he say to the idea of having an American for a son-in-law?

Nor was Mr. Ingram very lively. A young man when he has been just accepted, never is so. His happiness under the present circumstances was, no doubt, intense, but it was of a silent nature.

And then the interior of the building had to be visited. To tell the truth none of the party would have cared to perform this feat had it not been for the honour of the thing. To have come from Paris, New York, or London, to the Pyramids, and then not to have visited the very tomb of Cheops, would have shown on the part of all of them an indifference to subjects of interest which would have been altogether fatal to their character as travellers. And so a party for the interior was made up.

Miss Damer when she saw the aperture through which it was expected that she should descend, at once declared for staying with her mother. Miss Dawkins, however, was enthusiastic for the journey. 'Persons with so very little command over their nerves might really as well stay at home,' she said to Mr. Ingram, who glowered at her dreadfully for expressing such an opinion about his Fanny.

This entrance into the Pyramids is a terrible task, which should be undertaken by no lady. Those who perform it have to creep down, and then to be dragged up, through infinite dirt, foul smells, and bad air; and when they have done it, they see nothing. But they do earn the gratification of saying that they have been inside a Pyramid.

'Well, I've done that once,' said Mr. Damer, coming out, 'and I do not think that any one will catch me doing it again. I never was in such a filthy place in my life.'

'Oh, Fanny! I am so glad you did not go; I am sure it is not fit for ladies,' said poor Mrs. Damer, forgetful of her friend Miss Dawkins.

'I should have been ashamed of myself,' said Miss Dawkins, bristling up, and throwing back her head as she stood, 'if I had allowed any consideration to have prevented my visiting such a spot. If it be not improper for men to go there, how can it be improper for women?'

'I did not say improper, my dear,' said Mrs. Damer, apologetically.

'And as for the fatigue, what can a woman be worth who is afraid to encounter as much as I have now gone through for the sake of visiting the last resting-place of such a king as Cheops?' And Miss Dawkins, as she pronounced the last words, looked round her with disdain upon poor Fanny Damer.

'But I meant the dirt,' said Mrs. Damer.

'Dirt!' ejaculated Miss Dawkins, and then walked away. Why should she now submit her high tone of feeling to the Damers, or why care longer for their good opinion? Therefore she scattered contempt around her as she ejaculated the last word, 'dirt.'

And then the return home! 'I know I shall never get there,' said Mrs. Damer, looking piteously up into her husband's face.

'Nonsense, my dear; nonsense; you must get there.' Mrs. Damer groaned, and acknowleged in her heart that she must, – either dead or alive.

'And, Jefferson,' said Fanny, whispering – for there had been a moment since their descent in which she had been instructed to call him by his Christian name – 'never mind talking to me going home. I will ride by mamma. Do you go with papa and put him in good humour; and if he says anything about the lords and the bishops, don't you contradict him, you know.'

What will not a man do for love? Mr. Ingram promised. And in this way they started; the two boys led the van; then came Mr. Damer and Mr. Ingram, unusually and unpatriotically acquiescent as to England's aristocratic propensities; then Miss Dawkins riding, alas! alone; after her, M. Delabordeau, also alone, – the ungallant Frenchman! And the rear was brought up by Mrs. Damer and her daughter, flanked on each side by a dragoman, with a third dragoman behind them.

And in this order they went back to Cairo, riding their donkeys, and crossing the ferry solemnly, and, for the most part, silently. Mr. Ingram did talk, as he had an important object in view, – that of putting Mr. Damer into a good humour.

In this he succeeded so well that by the time they had remounted, after crossing the Nile, Mr. Damer opened his heart to his companion on the subject that was troubling him, and told him all about Miss Dawkins.

'I don't see why we should have a companion that we don't like for eight or ten weeks, merely because it seems rude to refuse a lady.'

'Indeed, I agree with you,' said Mr. Ingram; 'I should call it weak-minded to give way in such a case.'

'My daughter does not like her at all,' continued Mr. Damer.

'Nor would she be a nice companion for Miss Damer; not according to my way of thinking,' said Mr. Ingram.

'And as to my having asked her, or Mrs. Damer having asked her! Why God bless my soul, it is pure invention on the woman's part!'

'Ha! ha! ha!' laughed Mr. Ingram; 'I must say she plays her game well; but then she is an old soldier, and has the benefit of experience.' What would Miss Dawkins have said had she known that Mr. Ingram called her an old soldier?

'I don't like the kind of thing at all,' said Mr. Damer, who was very serious upon the subject. 'You see the position in which I am placed. I am forced to be very rude, or –'

'I don't call it rude at all.'

'Disobliging, then; or else I must have all my comfort invaded and pleasure destroyed by, by, by –' And Mr. Damer paused, being at a loss for an appropriate name for Miss Dawkins.

'By an unprotected female,' suggested Mr. Ingram.

'Yes; just so. I am as fond of pleasant company as anybody; but then I like to choose it myself.'

'So do I,' said Mr. Ingram, thinking of his own choice.

'Now, Ingram, if you would join us, we should be delighted.'

'Upon my word, sir, the offer is too flattering,' said Ingram, hesitatingly; for he felt that he could not undertake such a journey until Mr. Damer knew on what terms he stood with Fanny.

'You are a terrible democrat,' said Mr. Damer, laughing; 'but then, on that matter, you know, we could agree to differ.'

'Exactly so,' said Mr. Ingram, who had not collected his thoughts or made up his mind as to what he had better say and do, on the spur of the moment.

'Well what do you say to it?' said Mr. Damer, encouragingly. But Ingram paused before he answered.

'For Heaven's sake, my dear fellow, don't have the slightest hesitation in refusing, if you don't like the plan.'

'The fact is, Mr. Damer, I should like it too well.'

'Like it too well?'

'Yes, sir, and I may as well tell you now as later. I had intended this evening to have asked for your permission to address your daughter.'

'God bless my soul!' said Mr. Damer, looking as though a totally new idea had now been opened to him.

'And under these circumstances, I will now wait and see whether or no you will renew your offer.'

'God bless my soul!' said Mr. Damer again. It often does strike an old gentleman as very odd that any man should fall in love with his daughter, whom he has not ceased to look upon as a child. The case is generally quite different with mothers. They seem to think that every young man must fall in love with their girls.

'And have you said anything to Fanny about this?' asked Mr. Damer.

'Yes, sir, I have her permission to speak to you.'

'God bless my soul!' said Mr. Damer; and by this time they had arrived at Shepheard's Hotel.

'Oh, mamma,' said Fanny, as soon as she found herself alone with her mother that evening, 'I have something that I must tell you.'

'Oh, Fanny, don't tell me anything tonight, for I am a great deal too tired to listen.'

'But oh, mamma, pray; – you must listen to this; indeed you must.' And Fanny knelt down at her mother's knee, and looked beseechingly up into her face.

'What is it, Fanny? You know that all my bones are sore, and that I am so tired that I am almost dead.'

'Mamma, Mr. Ingram has –'

'Has what, my dear? has he done anything wrong?'

'No, mamma: but he has; – he has proposed to me.' And Fanny bursting into tears hid her face in her mother's lap.

And thus the story was told on both sides of the house. On the next day, as a matter of course, all the difficulties and dangers of such a marriage as that which was now projected were insisted on by both father and mother. It was improper; it would cause a severing of the family not to be thought of; it would be an alliance of a dangerous nature, and not at all calculated to insure happiness; and, in short, it was impossible. On that day, therefore, they all went to bed very unhappy. But on the next day, as was also a matter of course, seeing that there were no pecuniary difficulties, the mother and father were talked over, and Mr. Ingram was accepted as a

son-in-law. It need hardly be said that the offer of a place in
Mr. Damer's boat was again made, and that on this occasion it
was accepted without hesitation.

There was an American Protestant clergyman resident in
Cairo, with whom, among other persons, Miss Dawkins had
become acquainted. Upon this gentleman or upon his wife
Miss Dawkins called a few days after the journey to the
Pyramid, and finding him in his study, thus performed her
duty to her neighbour:

'You know your countryman Mr. Ingram, I think?' said
she.

'Oh, yes; very intimately.'

'If you have any regard for him, Mr. Burton,' such was the
gentleman's name, 'I think you should put him on his guard.'

'On his guard against what?' said Mr. Burton with a serious
air, for there was something serious in the threat of impending
misfortune as conveyed by Miss Dawkins.

'Why,' said she, 'those Damers, I fear, are dangerous
people.'

'Do you mean that they will borrow money of him?'

'Oh, no; not that exactly; but they are clearly setting their
cap at him.'

'Setting their cap at him?'

'Yes; there is a daughter, you know; a little chit of a thing:
and I fear Mr. Ingram may be caught before he knows where
he is. It would be such a pity, you know. He is going up the
river with them, I hear. That, in his place, is very foolish.
They asked me, but I positively refused.'

Mr. Burton remarked that 'in such a matter as that Mr.
Ingram would be perfectly able to take care of himself.'

'Well, perhaps so; but seeing what was going on, I thought
it my duty to tell you,' And so Miss Dawkins took her leave.

Mr. Ingram did go up the Nile with the Damers, as did an
old friend of the Damers who arrived from England. And a
very pleasant trip they had of it. And, as far as the present
historian knows, the two lovers were shortly afterwards
married in England.

Poor Miss Dawkins was left in Cairo for some time on her
beam ends. But she was one of those who are not easily
vanquished. After an interval of ten days she made acquaint-

ance with an Irish family – having utterly failed in moving the hard heart of M. Delabordeau – and with these she proceeded to Constantinople. They consisted of two brothers and a sister, and were, therefore, very convenient for matrimonial purposes. But nevertheless, when I last heard of Miss Dawkins, she was still an unprotected female.

THE O'CONORS OF CASTLE CONOR,
COUNTY MAYO

I shall never forget my first introduction to country life in Ireland, my first day's hunting there, or the manner in which I passed the evening afterwards. Nor shall I ever cease to be grateful for the hospitality which I received from the O'Conors of Castle Conor. My acquaintance with the family was first made in the following manner. But before I begin my story, let me inform my reader, that my name is Archibald Green.

I had been for a fortnight in Dublin, and was about to proceed into county Mayo on business which would occupy me there for some weeks. My headquarters would, I found, be at the town of Ballyglass; and I soon learned that Ballyglass was not a place in which I should find hotel accommodation of a luxurious kind, or much congenial society indigenous to the place itself.

'But you are a hunting man, you say,' said old Sir P—— C——; 'and in that case you will soon know Tom O'Conor. Tom won't let you be dull. I'd write you a letter to Tom, only he'll certainly make you out without my taking the trouble.'

I did think at the time that the old baronet might have written the letter for me, as he had been a friend of my father's in former days; but he did not, and I started for Ballyglass with no other introduction to any one in the county than that contained in Sir P——'s promise that I should soon know Mr. Thomas O'Conor.

I had already provided myself with a horse, groom, saddle and bridle, and these I sent down, en avant, that the Ballyglassians might know that I was somebody. Perhaps, before I arrived, Tom O'Conor might learn that a hunting man was coming into the neighbourhood, and I might find at the inn a polite note intimating that a bed was at my service at Castle Conor. I had heard so much of the free hospitality of the

Irish gentry as to imagine that such a thing might be possible.

But I found nothing of the kind. Hunting gentlemen in those days were very common in county Mayo, and one horse was no great evidence of a man's standing in the world. Men there, as I learnt afterwards, are sought for themselves quite as much as they are elsewhere; and though my groom's top-boots were neat, and my horse a very tidy animal, my entry into Ballyglass created no sensation whatever.

In about four days after my arrival, when I was already infinitely disgusted with the little pot-house in which I was forced to stay, and had made up my mind that the people in county Mayo were a churlish set, I sent my horse on to a meet of the fox-hounds, and followed after myself on an open car.

No one but an erratic fox-hunter such as I am – a fox-hunter, I mean, whose lot it has been to wander about from one pack of hounds to another – can understand the melancholy feeling which a man has when he first intrudes himself, unknown by any one, among an entirely new set of sportsmen. When a stranger falls thus, as it were out of the moon into a hunt, it is impossible that men should not stare at him and ask who he is. And it is so disagreeable to be stared at, and to have such questions asked! This feeling does not come upon a man in Leicestershire or Gloucestershire, where the numbers are large, and a stranger or two will always be overlooked, but in small hunting fields it is so painful that a man has to pluck up much courage before he encounters it.

We met on the morning in question at Bingham's Grove. There were not above twelve or fifteen men out, all of whom, or nearly all, were cousins to each other. They seemed to be all Toms, and Pats, and Larrys, and Micks. I was done up very knowingly in pink, and thought that I looked quite the thing; but for two or three hours nobody noticed me.

I had my eyes about me, however, and soon found out which of them was Tom O'Conor. He was a fine-looking fellow, thin and tall, but not largely made, with a piercing grey eye, and a beautiful voice for speaking to a hound. He had two sons there also, short, slight fellows, but exquisite horsemen. I already felt that I had a kind of acquaintance with the father, but I hardly knew on what ground to put in my claim.

We had no sport early in the morning. It was a cold bleak February day, with occasional storms of sleet. We rode from cover to cover, but all in vain. 'I am sorry, sir, that we are to have such a bad day, as you are a stranger here,' said one gentleman to me. This was Jack O'Conor, Tom's eldest son, my bosom friend for many a year after. Poor Jack! I fear that the Encumbered Estates Court sent him altogether adrift upon the world.

'We may still have a run from Poulnaroe, if the gentleman chooses to come on,' said a voice coming from behind with a sharp trot. It was Tom O'Conor.

'Wherever the hounds go, I'll follow,' said I.

'Then come on to Poulnaroe,' said Mr. O'Conor. I trotted on quickly by his side, and before we reached the cover, had managed to slip in something about Sir P.C.

'What the deuce!' said he. 'What! a friend of Sir P——'s? Why the deuce didn't you tell me so? What are you doing down here? Where are you staying,' &c., &c., &c.

At Poulnaroe we found a fox, but before we did so Mr. O'Conor had asked me over to Castle Conor. And this he did in such a way that there was no possibility of refusing him – or, I should rather say, of disobeying him. For his invitation came quite in the tone of a command.

'You'll come to us of course when the day is over – and let me see; we're near Ballyglass now, but the run will be right away in our direction. Just send word for them to send your things to Castle Conor.'

'But they're all about, and unpacked,' said I.

'Never mind. Write a note and say what you want now, and go and get the rest tomorrow yourself. Here. Patsey! – Patsey! run into Ballyglass for this gentleman at once. Now don't be long, for the chances are we shall find here.' And then, after giving some further hurried instructions he left me to write a line in pencil to the innkeeper's wife on the bank of a ditch.

This I accordingly did. 'Send my small portmanteau,' I said, 'and all my black dress clothes, and shirts, and socks, and all that, and above all my dressing things which are on the little table, and the satin neck-handkerchief, and whatever you do, mind you send my *pumps;*' and I underscored the latter word;

for Jack O'Conor, when his father left me, went on pressing the invitation. 'My sisters are going to get up a dance,' said he; 'and if you are fond of that kind of things perhaps we can amuse you.' Now in those days I was very fond of dancing – and very fond of young ladies too, and therefore glad enough to learn that Tom O'Conor had daughters as well as sons. On this account I was very particular in underscoring the word pumps.

'And hurry, you young divil,' he said to Patsey.

'I have told him to take the portmanteau over on a car,' said I.

'Alright; then you'll find it there on our arrival.'

We had an excellent run in which I may make bold to say that I did not acquit myself badly. I stuck very close to the hounds, as did the whole of the O'Conor brood; and when the fellow contrived to earth himself, as he did, I received those compliments on my horse, which is the most approved praise which one fox-hunter ever gives to another.

'We'll buy that fellow off you before we let you go,' said Peter, the youngest son.

'I advise you to look sharp after your money if you sell him to my brother,' said Jack.

And then we trotted slowly off to Castle Conor, which, however, was by no means near to us. 'We have ten miles to go; – good Irish miles,' said the father. 'I don't know that I ever remember a fox from Poulnaroe taking that line before.'

'He wasn't a Poulnaroe fox,' said Peter.

'I don't know that,' said Jack; and then they debated that question hotly.

Our horses were very tired, and it was late before we reached Mr. O'Conor's house. That getting home from hunting with a thoroughly weary animal, who has no longer sympathy or example to carry him on, is very tedious work. In the present instance I had company with me; but when a man is alone, when his horse toes at every ten steps, when the night is dark and the rain pouring, and there are yet eight miles of road to be conquered, – at such times a man is almost apt to swear that he will give up hunting.

At last we were in the Castle Conor stable yard; – for we had approached the house by some back way; and as we

entered the house by a door leading through a wilderness of
back passages, Mr. O'Conor said out loud, 'Now, boys,
remember I sit down to dinner in twenty minutes.' And then
turning expressly to me, he laid his hand kindly upon my
shoulder and said, 'I hope you will make yourself quite at home
at Castle Conor, – and whatever you do, don't keep us waiting
for dinner. You can dress in twenty minutes, I suppose?'

'In ten!' said I, glibly.

'That's well. Jack and Peter will show you your room,' and
so he turned away and left us.

My two young friends made their way into the great hall,
and thence into the drawing-room, and I followed them. We
were all dressed in pink, and had waded deep through bog and
mud. I did not exactly know whither I was being led in this
guise, but I soon found myself in the presence of two young
ladies, and of a girl about thirteen years of age.

'My sisters,' said Jack, introducing me very laconically;
'Miss O'Conor, Miss Kate O'Conor, Miss Tizzy O'Conor.'

'My name is not Tizzy,' said the younger; 'it's Eliza. How
do you do, sir? I hope you had a fine hunt! Was papa well up,
Jack?'

Jack did not condescend to answer this question, but asked
one of the elder girls whether anything had come, and
whether a room had been made ready for me.

'Oh yes!' said Miss O'Conor; 'they came, I know, for I saw
them brought into the house; and I hope Mr. Green will find
everything comfortable.' As she said this I thought I saw a
slight smile steal across her remarkably pretty mouth.

They were both exceedingly pretty girls. Fanny the elder
wore long glossy curls, – for I write, oh reader, of bygone
days, as long ago as that, when ladies wore curls if it pleased
them so to do, and gentlemen danced in pumps, with black
handkerchiefs round their necks – yes, long black, or nearly
black silken curls; and then she had such eyes; – I never knew
whether they were most wicked or most bright; and her face
was all dimples, and each dimple was laden with laughter and
laden with love. Kate was probably the prettier girl of the
two, but on the whole not so attractive. She was fairer than
her sister, and wore her hair in braids; and was also somewhat
more demure in her manner.

In spite of the special injunctions of Mr. O'Conor senior, it was impossible not to loiter for five minutes over the drawing-room fire talking to these houris – more especially as I seemed to know them intimately by intuition before half of the five minutes was over. They were so easy, so pretty, so graceful, so kind, they seemed to take it so much as a matter of course that I should stand there talking in my red coat and muddy boots.

'Well; do go and dress youselves,' at last said Fanny, pretending to speak to her brothers but looking more especially at me 'You know how mad papa will be. And remember, Mr. Green, we expect great things from your dancing tonight. Your coming just at this time is such a Godsend.' And again that soupçon of a smile passed over her face.

I hurried up to my room. Peter and Jack coming with me to the door. 'Is everything right?' said Peter, looking among the towels and water-jugs. They've given you a decent fire for a wonder,' said Jack stirring up the red hot turf which blazed in the grate. 'All right as a trivet,' said I. 'And look alive like a good fellow,' said Jack. We had scowled at each other in the morning as very young men do when they are strangers; and now, after a few hours, we were intimate friends.

I immediately turned to my work, and was gratified to find that all my things were laid out ready for dressing; my portmanteau had of course come open, as my keys were in my pocket, and therefore some of the excellent servants of the house had been able to save me all the trouble of unpacking. There was my shirt hanging before the fire; my black clothes were spread upon the bed, my socks and collar and handkerchief beside them; my brushes were on the toilet table, and everything prepared exactly as though my own man had been there. How nice.

I immediately went to work at getting off my spurs and boots, and then proceeded to loosen the buttons at my knees. In doing this I sat down in the arm-chair which had been drawn up for me, opposite the fire. But what was the object on which my eyes then fell; – the objects I should rather say!

Immediately in front of my chair was placed, just ready for my feet, an enormous pair of shooting-boots – half-boots, made to lace up round the ankles, with thick double leather soles, and each bearing half a stone of iron in the shape of nails and heel-pieces. I had superintended the making of these shoes in Burlington Arcade with the greatest diligence. I was never a good shot; and, like some other sportsmen, intended to make up for my deficiency in performance by the excellence of my shooting apparel. 'Those nails are not large enough,' I had said; 'nor nearly large enough.' But when the boots came home they struck even me as being too heavy, too metalsome. 'He, he, he,' laughed the boot boy as he turned them up for me to look at. It may therefore be imagined of what nature were the articles which were thus set out for the evening's dancing.

And then the way in which they were placed! When I saw this the conviction flew across my mind like a flash of lightning that the preparation had been made under other eyes than those of the servant. The heavy big boots were placed so prettily before the chair, and the strings of each were made to dangle down at the sides, as though just ready for tying! They seemed to say, the boots did, 'Now make haste. We at any rate are ready – you cannot say that you were kept waiting for us.' No mere servant's hand had ever enabled a pair of boots to laugh at one so completely.

But what was I to do? I rushed at the small portmanteau, thinking that my pumps also might be there. The woman surely could not have been such a fool as to send me those tons of iron for my evening wear! But alas, alas! no pumps were there. There was nothing else in the way of covering for my feet; not even a pair of slippers.

And now what was I to do? The absolute magnitude of my misfortune only loomed upon me by degrees. The twenty mintues allowed by that stern old paterfamilias were already gone and I had done nothing towards dressing. And indeed it was impossible that I should do anything that would be of avail. I could not go down to dinner in my stocking feet, nor could I put on my black dress trousers over a pair of mud painted top-boots. As for those iron-soled horrors –; and then I gave one of them a kick with the side of my bare foot which sent it half way under the bed.

But what was I to do? I began washing myself and brushing my hair with this horrid weight upon my mind. My first plan was to go to bed, and send down word that I had been taken suddenly ill in the stomach; then to rise early in the morning and get· away unobserved. But by such a course of action I should lose all chance of any further acquaintance with those pretty girls! That they were already aware of the extent of my predicament, and were now enjoying it – of that I was quite sure.

What if I boldly put on the shooting-boots, and clattered down to dinner in them? What if I took the bull by the horns, and made myself the most of the joke? This might be very well for the dinner, but it would be a bad joke for me when the hour for dancing came. And, alas! I felt that I lacked the courage. It is not every man that can walk down to dinner, in a strange house full of ladies, wearing such boots as those I have described.

Should I not attempt to borrow a pair? This, all the world will say, should have been my first idea. But I have not yet mentioned that I am myself a large-boned man, and that my feet are especially well developed. I had never for a moment entertained a hope that I should find any one in that house whose boot I could wear. But at last I rang the bell. I would send for Jack, and if everything failed, I would communicate my grief to him.

I had to ring twice before anybody came. The servants, I well knew, were putting the dinner on the table. At last a man entered the room, dressed in rather shabby black, whom I afterwards learned to be the butler.

'What is your name, my friend,' said I, determined to make an ally of the man.

'My name? Why Larry sure, yer honor. And the masther is out of his sinses in a hurry, because yer honer don't come down.'

'Is he though? Well, now Larry; tell me this; which of all the gentlemen in the house has got the largest foot?'

'Is it the largest foot, yer honer?' said Larry, altogether surprised by my question.

'Yes, the largest foot,' and then I proceeded to explain to him my misfortune. He took up first my top-boot, and then the shooting-boot – in looking at which he gazed with wonder at the nails; – and then he glanced at my feet, measuring them with his eye; and after this he pronounced his opinion.

'Yer honer couldn't wear a morsel of leather belonging to ere a one of 'em, young or ould. There niver was a foot like that yet among the O'Conors.'

'But are there no strangers staying here?'

'There's three or four on 'em come in to dinner; but they'll be wanting their own boots I'm thinking. And there's young Mister Dillon; he's come to stay. But Lord love you –' and he again looked at the enormous extent which lay between the heel and the toe of the shooting apparatus which he still held in his hand. 'I niver see such a foot as that in the whole barony,' he said, 'barring my own.'

Now Larry was a large man, much larger altogether than myself, and as he said this I looked down involuntarily at his feet; or rather at his foot, for as he stood I could only see one. And then a sudden hope filled my heart. On that foot there glittered a shoe – not indeed such as were my own which were now resting ingloriously at Ballyglass while they were so sorely needed at Castle Conor; but one which I could wear before ladies, without shame – and in my present frame of mind with infinite contentment.

'Let me look at that one of your own,' said I to the man, as though it were merely a subject for experimental inquiry. Larry, accustomed to obedience, took off the shoe and handed it to me. My own foot was immediately in it, and I found that it fitted me like a glove.

'And now the other,' said I – not smiling, for a smile would have put him on his guard; but somewhat sternly, so that that habit of obedience should not desert him at this perilous moment. And then I stretched out my hand.

'But yer honer can't keep 'em, you know,' said he. 'I haven't the ghost of another shoe to my feet.' But I only looked more sternly than before, and still held out my hand. Custom prevailed. Larry stooped down slowly, looking at me the while, and pulling off the other slipper handed it to me with much hesitation. Alas! as I put it to my foot I found that it was old, and worn, and irredeemably down at heel; – that it was in fact no counterpart at all to that other one which was to do duty as its fellow. But nevertheless I put my foot into it, and felt that a descent to the drawing-room was now possible.

'But yer honer will give 'em back to a poor man?' said Larry almost crying. 'The masther's mad this minute because the dinner's not up. Glory to God, only listen to that.' And as he spoke a tremendous peal rang out from some bell down stairs that had evidently been shaken by an angry hand.

'Larry,' said I – and I endeavoured to assume a look of very grave importance as I spoke – 'I look to you to assist me in this matter.'

'Och – wirra sthrue then, and will you let me go? just listen to that,' and another angry peal rang out, loud and repeated.

'If you do as I ask you,' I continued, 'you shall be well rewarded. Look here; look at these boots,' and I held up the shooting-shoes new from Burlington Arcade. 'They cost thirty shillings – thirty shillings! and I will give them to you for the loan of this pair of slippers.'

'They'd be no use at all to me, yer honer; not the laist use in life.'

'You could do with them very well for tonight, and then you could sell them. And here are ten shillings besides,' and I held out half a sovereign which the poor fellow took into his hand.

I waited no further parley but immediately walked out of the room. With one foot I was sufficiently pleased. As regarded that I felt that I had overcome my difficulty. But the other was not so satisfactory. Whenever I attempted to lift it from the ground the horrid slipper would fall off, or only just hang by the toe. As for dancing, that would be out of the question.

'Och, murther, murther,' sang out Larry, as he heard me going down stairs. 'What will I do at all? Tare and 'ounds; there, he's at it agin, as mad as blazes.' This last exclamation had reference to another peal which was evidently the work of the master's hand.

I confess I was not quite comfortable as I walked down stairs. In the first place I was nearly half an hour late, and I knew from the vigour of the peals that had sounded that my slowness had already been made the subject of strong remarks. And then my left shoe went flop, flop on every alternate step of the stairs; by no exertion of my foot in the drawing up of my toe could I induce it to remain permanently fixed upon my foot. But over and above and worse than all this was the conviction strong upon my mind that I should become a subject of merriment to the girls as soon as I entered the room. They would understand the cause of my distress, and probably at this moment were expecting to hear me clatter through the stone hall with those odious metal boots.

However, I hurried down and entered the drawing-room, determined to keep my position near the door, so that I might have as little as possible to do on entering and as little as possible in going out. But I had other difficulties in store for me. I had not as yet been introduced to Mrs. O'Conor; nor to Miss O'Conor, the squire's unmarried sister.

'Upon my word I thought you were never coming,' said Mr. O'Conor as soon as he saw me. 'It is just one hour since we entered the house. Jack, I wish you would find out what has come to that fellow Larry,' and again he rang the bell. He was too angry, or it might be too impatient to go through the ceremony of introducing me to anybody.

I saw that the two girls looked at me very sharply, but I stood at the back of an arm-chair so that no one could see my feet. But that little imp Tizzy walked round deliberately, looked at my heels, and then walked back again. It was clear that she was in the secret.

There were eight or ten people in the room, but I was too much fluttered to notice well who they were.

'Mamma,' said Miss O'Conor, 'let me introduce Mr. Green to you.'

It luckily happened that Mrs. O'Conor was on the same side of the fire as myself, and I was able to take the hand which she offered me without coming round into the middle of the circle. Mrs. O'Conor was a little woman, apparently not of much importance in the world, but, if one might judge from first appearance, very good-natured.

'And my aunt Die, Mr. Green,' said Kate, pointing to a very straight-backed, grim-looking lady, who occupied a corner of a sofa, on the opposite side of the hearth. I knew that politeness required that I should walk across the room and make acquaintance with her. But under the existing circumstances how was I to obey the dictates of politeness? I was determined therefore to stand my ground, and merely bowed across the room at Miss O'Conor. In so doing I made an enemy who never deserted me during the whole of my intercourse with the family. But for her, who knows who might have been sitting opposite to me as I now write?

'Upon my word, Mr. Green, the ladies will expect much from an Adonis who takes so long over his toilet,' said Tom O'Conor in that cruel tone of banter which he knew so well how to use.

'You forget, father, that men in London can't jump in and out of their clothes as quick as we wild Irishmen,' said Jack.

'Mr. Green knows that we expect a great deal from him this evening. I hope you polk well, Mr. Green,' said Kate.

I muttered something about never dancing, but I knew that that which I said was inaudible.

'I don't think Mr. Green will dance,' said Tizzy; 'at least not much.' The impudence of that child was, I think, unparalleled by any that I have ever witnessed.

'But in the name of all that's holy, why don't we have dinner?' And Mr. O'Conor thundered at the door. 'Larry, Larry, Larry!' he screamed.

'Yes, yer honer, it'll be all right in two seconds,' answered Larry, from some bottomless abyss. 'Tare an' ages; what'll I do at all,' I heard him continuing, as he made his way into the hall. Oh what a clatter he made upon the pavement, – for it was all stone! And how the drops of perspiration stood upon my brow as I listened to him!

And then there was a pause, for the man had gone into the dining-room. I could see now that Mr. O'Conor was becoming very angry, and Jack the eldest son – oh, how often he and I have laughed over all this since – left the drawing-room for the second time. Immediately afterwards, Larry's footsteps were again heard, hurrying across the hall, and then there was a great slither, and an exclamation, and the noise of a fall – and I could plainly hear poor Larry's head strike against the stone floor.

'Ochone, ochone!' he cried at the top of his voice – 'I'm murthered with 'em now intirely; and d—— 'em for boots – St. Peter be good to me.'

There was a general rush into the hall, and I was carried with the stream. The poor fellow who had broken his head would be sure to tell how I had robbed him of his shoes. The coachman was already helping him up, and Peter good-naturedly lent a hand.

'What on earth is the matter?' said Mr. O'Conor.

'He must be tipsy,' whispered Miss O'Conor, the maiden sister.

'I aint tipsy at all thin,' said Larry, getting up and rubbing the back of his head, and sundry other parts of his body. 'Tipsy indeed!' And then he added when he was quite upright, 'The dinner is sarved – at last.'

And he bore it all without telling. 'I'll give that fellow a guinea tomorrow morning,' said I to myself – 'if it's the last that I have in the world.'

I shall never forget the countenance of the Miss O'Conors as Larry scrambled up cursing the unfortunate boots – 'What on earth has he got on,' said Mr. O'Conor.

'Sorrow take 'em for shoes,' ejaculated Larry. But his spirit was good and he said not a word to betray me.

We all then went in to dinner how we best could. It was useless for us to go back into the drawing-room, that each might seek his own partner. Mr. O'Conor 'the masther,' not caring much for the girls who were around him, and being already half beside himself with the confusion and delay, led the way by himself. I as a stranger should have given my arm to Mrs. O'Conor; but as it was I took her eldest daughter instead, and contrived to shuffle along into the dining-room without exciting much attention, and when there I found myself happily placed between Kate and Fanny.

'I never knew anything so awkward,' said Fanny; 'I declare I can't conceive what has come to our old servant Larry. He's generally the most precise person in the world, and now he is nearly an hour late – and then he tumbles down in the hall.'

'I am afraid I am responsible for the delay,' said I.

'But not for the tumble I suppose,' said Kate from the other side. I felt that I blushed up to the eyes, but I did not dare to enter into explanations.

'Tom,' said Tizzy, addressing her father across the table, 'I hope you had a good run today.' It did seem odd to me that a young lady should call her father Tom, but such was the fact.

'Well; pretty well,' said Mr. O'Conor.

'And I hope you were up with the hounds.'

'You may ask Mr. Green that. He at any rate was with them, and therefore he can tell you.'

'Oh, he wasn't before you, I know. No Englishman could get before you – I am quite sure of that.'

'Don't you be impertinent, miss,' said Kate. 'You can easily see, Mr. Green, that papa spoils my sister Eliza.'

'Do you hunt in top-boots, Mr. Green?' said Tizzy.

To this I made no answer. She would have drawn me into a conversation about my feet in half a minute, and the slightest allusion to the subject threw me into a fit of perspiration.

'Are you fond of hunting, Miss O'Conor?' asked I, blindly hurrying into any other subject of conversation.

Miss O'Conor owned that she was fond of hunting – just a little; only papa would not allow it. When the hounds met anywhere within reach of Castle Conor, she and Kate would ride out to look at them; and if papa was not there that day – an omission of rare occurrence – they would ride a few fields with the hounds.

'But he lets Tizzy keep with them the whole day,' said she whispering.

'And has Tizzy a pony of her own?'

'Oh yes, Tizzy has everything. She's papa's pet, you know.'

'And whose pet are you?' I asked.

'Oh – I am nobody's pet, unless sometimes Jack makes a pet of me when he's in a good humour. Do you make pets of your sisters, Mr. Green?'

'I have none. But if I had I should not make pets of them.'

'Not of your own sisters?'

'No. As for myself I'd sooner make a pet of my friend's sister; a great deal.'

'How very unnatural,' said Miss O'Conor with the prettiest look of surprise imaginable.

'Not at all unnatural I think,' said I, looking tenderly and lovingly into her face. Where does one find girls so pretty, so easy, so sweet, so talkative as the Irish girls? And then with all their talking and all their ease, who ever hears of their misbehaving? They certainly love flirting as they also love dancing. But they flirt without mischief and without malice.

I had now quite forgotten my misfortune, and was beginning to think how well I should like to have Fanny O'Conor for my wife. In this frame of mind I was bending over towards her as a servant took away a plate from the other side, when a sepulchral note sounded in my ear. It was like the memento mori of the old Roman; – as though some one pointed in the midst of my bliss to the sword hung over my head by a thread. It was the voice of Larry, whispering in his agony just above my head –

'They's disthroying my poor feet intirely, intirely; so they is! I can't bear it much longer, yer honer.' I had committed murder like Macbeth; and now my Banquo had come to disturb me at my feast.

'What is it he says to you?' asked Fanny.

'Oh nothing,' I answered, once more in my misery.

'There seems to be some point of confidence between you and our Larry,' she remarked.

'Oh no,' said I, quite confused; 'not at all.'

'You need not be ashamed of it. Half the gentlemen in the county have their confidences with Larry; – and some of the ladies too, I can tell you. He was born in this house, and never lived anywhere else; and I am sure he has a larger circle of acquaintance than any one else in it.'

I could not recover my self-possession for the next ten minutes. Whenever Larry was on our side of the table I was afraid he was coming to me with another agonized whisper. When he was opposite I could not but watch him as he hobbled in his misery. It was evident that the boots were too tight for him, and had they been made throughout of iron they could not have been less capable of yielding to the feet. I pitied him from the bottom of my heart. And I pitied myself also, wishing that I was well in bed upstairs with some feigned malady, so that Larry might have had his own again.

And then for a moment I missed him from the room. He had doubtless gone to relieve his tortured feet in the servants-hall, and as he did so was cursing my cruelty. But what mattered it? Let him curse. If he would only stay away and do that I would appease his wrath when we were alone together with pecuniary satisfaction.

But there was no such rest in store for me. 'Larry, Larry,' shouted Mr. O'Conor, 'where on earth has the fellow gone to?' They were all cousins at the table except myself, and Mr. O'Conor was not therefore restrained by any feeling of ceremony. 'There is something wrong with that fellow today; what is it, Jack?'

'Upon my word, sir, I don't know,' said Jack.

'I think he must be tipsy,' whispered Miss O'Conor, the maiden sister, who always sat at her brother's left hand. But a whisper though it was, it was audible all down the table.

'No, ma'am; it aint dhrink at all,' said the coachman. 'It is his feet as does it.'

'His feet!' shouted Tom O'Conor.

'Yes; I know it's his feet,' said that horrid Tizzy. 'He's got on great thick nailed shoes. It was that that made him tumble down in the hall.'

I glanced at each side of me, and could see that there was a certain consciousness expressed in the face of each of my two neighbours; – on Kate's mouth there was decidedly a smile, or rather perhaps the slightest possible inclination that way; whereas on Fanny's part I thought I saw something like a rising sorrow at my distress. So at least I flattered myself.

'Send him back into the room immediately,' said Tom, who looked at me as though he had some consciousness that I had introduced all this confusion into his household. What should I do? Would it not be best for me to make a clean breast of it before them all? But alas! I lacked the courage.

The coachman went out, and we were left for five minutes without any servant, and Mr. O'Conor the while became more and more savage. I attempted to say a word to Fanny, but failed – Vox faucibus hæsit.

'I don't think he has got any others,' said Tizzy – 'at least none others left.'

On the whole I am glad I did not marry into the family, as I could not have endured that girl to stay in my house as a sister-in-law.

'Where the d—— has that other fellow gone to?' said Tim. 'Jack, do go out and see what is the matter. If anybody is drunk send for me.'

'Oh, there is nobody drunk,' said Tizzy.

Jack went out, and the coachman returned; but what was done and said I hardly remember. The whole room seemed to swim round and round, and as far as I can recollect the company sat mute, neither eating nor drinking. Presently Jack returned.

'It's all right,' said he. I always liked Jack. At the present moment he just looked towards me and laughed slightly.

'All right?' said Tom. 'But is the fellow coming?'

'We can do with Richard, I suppose,' said Jack.

'No – I can't do with Richard,' said the father. 'And I will know what it all means. Where is that fellow Larry?'

Larry had been standing just outside the door, and now he entered gently as a mouse. No sound came from his footfall, nor was there in his face that look of pain which it had worn for the last fifteen minutes. But he was not the less abashed, frightened, and unhappy.

'What is all this about, Larry?' said his master, turning to him. 'I insist upon knowing.'

'Och thin, Mr. Green, yer honer, I wouldn't be afther telling agin yer honer; indeed I wouldn't thin, av' the masther would only let me hould my tongue.' And he looked across at me, deprecating my anger.

'Mr. Green!' said Mr. O'Conor.

'Yes, yer honer. Its all along of his honer's thick shoes,' and Larry stepping backwards towards the door, lifted them up from some corner, and coming well foward, exposed them with the soles uppermost to the whole table.

'And that's not all, yer honer; but they've squoze the very toes of me into a jelly.'

There was now a loud laugh, in which Jack and Peter and Fanny and Kate and Tizzy all joined; as too did Mr. O'Conor – and I also myself after a while.

'Whose boots are they?' demanded Miss O'Conor senior, with her severest tone and grimmest accent.

''Deed then and the divil may have them for me, Miss,' answered Larry. 'They war Mr. Green's, but the likes of him won't wear them agin afther the likes of me – barring he wanted them very particular,' added he, remembering his own pumps.

I began muttering something, feeling that the time had come when I must tell the tale. But Jack with great good nature, took up the story and told it so well, that I hardly suffered in the telling.

'And that's it,' said Tom O'Conor, laughing till I thought he would have fallen from his chair. 'So you've got Larry's shoes on –'

'And very well he fills them,' said Jack.

'And it's his honer that's welcome to 'em,' said Larry, grinning from ear to ear now that he saw that 'the masther' was once more in a good humour.

'I hope they'll be nice shoes for dancing,' said Kate.

'Only there's one down at the heel I know,' said Tizzy.

'The servant's shoes!' This was an exclamation made by the maiden lady, and intended apparently only for her brother's ear. But it was clearly audible by all the party.

'Better that than no dinner,' said Peter.

'But what are you to do about the dancing?' said Fanny, with an air of dismay on her face which flattered me with an idea that she did care whether I danced or no.

In the mean time Larry, now as happy as an emperor, was tripping round the room without any shoes to encumber him as he withdrew the plates from the table.

'And it's his honer that's welcome to 'em,' said he again, as he pulled off the table-cloth with a flourish. 'And why wouldn't he, and he able to folly the hounds betther nor any Englishman that iver war in these parts before, – anyways so Mick says!'

Now Mick was the huntsman, and this little tale of eulogy from Larry went far towards easing my grief. I had ridden well to the hounds that day, and I knew it.

There was nothing more said about the shoes, and I was soon again at my ease, although Miss O'Conor did say something about the impropriety of Larry walking about in his stocking feet. The ladies however soon withdrew, – to my sorrow, for I was getting on swimmingly with Fanny; and then we gentlemen gathered round the fire and filled our glasses.

In about ten mintues a very light tap was heard, the door was opened to the extent of three inches, and a female voice which I readily recognized called to Jack.

Jack went out, and in a second or two put his head back into the room and called to me – 'Green,' he said, 'just step here a moment, there's a good fellow.' I went out, and there I found Fanny standing with her brother.

'Here are the girls at their wits' ends,' said he, 'about your dancing. So Fanny has put a boy upon one of the horses, and proposes that you should send another line to Mrs. Meehan at Ballyglass. It's only ten miles, and he'll be back in two hours.'

I need hardly say that I acted in conformity with this advice. I went into Mr. O'Conor's book room, with Jack and his sister, and there scribbled a note. It was delightful to feel how intimate I was with them and how anxious they were to make me happy.

'And we won't begin till they come,' said Fanny.

'Oh, Miss O'Conor, pray don't wait,' said I.

'Oh, but we will,' she answered. 'You have your wine to drink, and then there's the tea; and then we'll have a song or two. I'll spin it out; see if I don't.' And so we went to the front door where the boy was already on his horse – her own nag as I afterwards found.

'And Patsey,' said she, 'ride for your life now; and Patsey, whatever you do, don't come back without Mr. Green's pumps – his dancing-shoes you know.'

And in about two hours the pumps did arrive; and I don't think I ever spent a pleasanter evening or got more satisfaction out of a pair of shoes. They had not been two minutes on my feet before Larry was carrying a tray of negus across the room in those which I had worn at dinner.

'The Dillon girls are going to stay here,' said Fanny as I wished her good night at two o'clock. 'And we'll have dancing every evening as long as you remain.'

'But I shall leave tomorrow,' said I.

'Indeed you won't. Papa will take care of that.'

And so he did. 'You had better go over to Ballyglass yourself tomorrow,' said he, 'and collect your own things. There's no knowing else what you may have to borrow of Larry.'

I stayed there three weeks, and in the middle of the third I thought that everything would be arranged between me and Fanny. But the aunt interfered; and in about a twelvemonth after my adventures she consented to make a more fortunate man happy for his life.

THE MISTLETOE BOUGH

'Let the boys have it if they like it,' said Mrs. Garrow, pleading to her only daughter on behalf of her two sons.

'Pray don't, mamma,' said Elizabeth Garrow. 'It only means romping. To me all that is detestable, and I am sure it is not the sort of thing that Miss Holmes would like.'

'We always had it at Christmas when we were young.'

'But, mamma, the world is so changed.'

The point in dispute was one very delicate in its nature, hardly to be discussed in all its bearings, even in fiction, and the very mention of which between a mother and daughter showed a great amount of close confidence between them. It was no less than this. Should that branch of mistletoe which Frank Garrow had brought home with him out of the Lowther woods be hung up on Christmas Eve in the dining-room at Thwaite Hall, according to his wishes; or should permission for such hanging be positively refused? It was clearly a thing not to be done after such a discussion, and therefore the decision given by Mrs. Garrow was against it.

I am inclined to think that Miss Garrow was right in saying that the world is changed as touching mistletoe boughs. Kissing, I fear, is less innocent now than it used to be when our grandmothers were alive, and we have become more fastidious in our amusements. Nevertheless, I think that she made herself fairly open to the raillery with which her brothers attacked her.

'Honi soit qui mal y pense,' said Frank, who was eighteen.

'Nobody will want to kiss you, my lady Fineairs,' said Harry, who was just a year younger.

'Because you choose to be a Puritan, there are to be no more cakes and ale in the house,' said Frank.

'Still waters run deep; we all know that,' said Harry.

The boys had not been present when the matter was decided between Mrs. Garrow and her daughter, nor had the mother been present when these little amenities had passed between the brothers and sister.

'Only that mamma has said it, and I wouldn't seem to go against her,' said Frank, 'I'd ask my father. He wouldn't give way to such nonsense, I know.'

Elizabeth turned away without answering, and left the room. Her eyes were full of tears, but she would not let them see that they had vexed her. They were only two days home from school, and for the last week before their coming, all her thoughts had been to prepare for their Christmas pleasures. She had arranged their rooms, making everything warm and pretty. Out of her own pocket she had bought a shot-belt for one, and skates for the other. She had told the old groom that her pony was to belong exclusively to Master Harry for the holidays, and now Harry told her that still waters ran deep. She had been driven to the use of all her eloquence in inducing her father to purchase that gun for Frank, now Frank called her Puritan. And why? She did not choose that a mistletoe bough should be hung in her father's hall, when Godfrey Holmes was coming to visit him. She could not explain this to Frank, but Frank might have had the wit to understand it. But Frank was thinking only of Patty Coverdale, a blue-eyed little romp of sixteen, who with her sister Kate, was coming from Penrith to spend the Christmas at Thwaite Hall. Elizabeth left the room with her slow, graceful step, hiding her tears, – hiding all emotion, as latterly she had taught herself that it was feminine to do. 'There goes my lady Fineairs,' said Harry, sending his shrill voice after her.

Thwaite Hall was not a place of much pretension. It was a moderate-sized house, surrounded by pretty gardens and shrubberies, close down upon the river Eamont, on the Westmoreland side of the river, looking over to a lovely wooded bank in Cumberland. All the world knows that the Eamont runs out of Ulleswater, dividing the two counties, passing under Penrith Bridge and by the old ruins of Brougham Castle, below which it joins the Eden. Thwaite Hall nestled down close upon the clear rocky stream about half way between Ulleswater and Penrith, and had been built just at a bend of the river. The windows of the dining-parlour and of the drawing-room stood at right angles to each other, and yet each commanded a reach of the stream. Immediately from a side door of the house steps were cut down through the red rock to the water's edge, and here a small boat was always moored to a chain. The chain was stretched across the river, fixed to the staples driven into the rock on either side, and the boat was pulled backwards and forwards over the stream without aid from oars or paddles. From the opposite side a path led through the woods and across the fields to Penrith, and this was the route commonly used between Thwaite Hall and the town.

Major Garrow was a retired officer of Engineers, who had seen service in all parts of the world, and who was now spending the evening of his days on a small property which had come to him from his father. He held in his own hands about twenty acres of land, and he was the owner of one small farm close by, which was let to a tenant. That, together with his half-pay, and the interest of his wife's thousand pounds, sufficed to educate his children and keep the wolf at a comfortable distance from his door. He himself was a spare thin man, with quiet, lazy, literary habits. He had done the work of life, but had so done it as to permit of his enjoying that which was left to him. His sole remaining care was the establishment of his children; and, as far as he could see, he had no ground for anticipating disappointment. They were clever, good-looking, well-disposed young people, and upon the whole it may be said that the sun shone brightly on Thwaite Hall. Of Mrs. Garrow it may suffice to say that she always deserved such sunshine.

For years past it had been the practice of the family to have some sort of gathering at Thwaite Hall during Christmas. Godfrey Holmes had been left under the guardianship of Major Garrow, and, as he had always spent his Christmas holidays with his guardian, this, perhaps, had given rise to the practice. Then the Coverdales were cousins of the Garrows, and they had usually been there as children. At the Christmas last past the custom had been broken, for young Holmes had been abroad. Previous to that, they had all been children, excepting him. But now that they were to meet again, they were no longer children. Elizabeth, at any rate, was not so, for she had already counted nineteen winters. And Isabella

Holmes was coming. Now Isabella was two years older than
Elizabeth, and had been educated in Brussels; moreover she
was comparatively a stranger at Thwaite Hall, never having
been at those early Christmas meetings.

And now I must take permission to begin my story by
telling a lady's secret. Elizabeth Garrow had already been in
love with Godfrey Holmes, or perhaps it might be more
becoming to say that Godfrey Holmes had already been in
love with her. They had already been engaged; and, alas! they
had already agreed that that engagement should be broken off!

Young Holmes was now twenty-seven years of age, and
was employed in a bank at Liverpool, not as a clerk, but as
assistant manager, with a large salary. He was a man well to
do in the world, who had money also of his own, and who
might well afford to marry. Some two years since, on the eve
of leaving Thwaite Hall, he had with low doubting whisper
told Elizabeth that he loved her, and she had flown trembling
to her mother. 'Godfrey, my boy,' the father said to him, as
he parted with him the next morning, 'Bessy is only a child,
and too young to think of this yet.' At the next Christmas
Godfrey was in Italy, and the thing was gone by, – so at least
the father and mother said to each other. But the young
people had met in the summer, and one joyful letter had come
from the girl home to her mother. 'I have accepted him.
Dearest, dearest mamma, I do love him. But don't tell papa
yet, for I have not quite accepted him. I think I am sure, but I
am not quite sure. I am not quite sure about him.'

And then, two days after that, there had come a letter that
was not at all joyful. 'Dearest Mamma, – It is not to be. It is
not written in the book. We have both agreed that it will not
do. I am so glad that you have not told dear papa, for I could
never make him understand. You will understand, for I shall
tell you everything, down to his very words. But we have
agreed that there shall be no quarrel. It shall be exactly as it
was, and he will come at Christmas all the same. It would
never do that he and papa should be separated, nor could we
now put off Isabella. It is better so in every way, for there is
and need be no quarrel. We still like each other. I am sure I like
him, but I know that I should not make him happy as his wife.
He says it is my fault. I, at any rate, have never told him that I

thought it his.' From all which it will be seen that the confidence between the mother and daughter was very close.

Elizabeth Garrow was a very good girl, but it might almost be a question whether she was not too good. She had learned, or thought that she had learned, that most girls are vapid, silly, and useless, – given chiefly to pleasure-seeking and a hankering after lovers; and she had resolved that she would not be such a one. Industry, self-denial, and a religious purpose in life, were the tasks which she set herself; and she went about the performance of them with much courage. But such tasks, though they are excellently well adapted to fit a young lady for the work of living, may also be carried too far, and thus have the effect of unfitting her for that work. When Elizabeth Garrow made up her mind that the finding of a husband was not the only purpose of life, she did very well. It is very well that a young lady should feel herself capable of going through the world happily without one. But in teaching herself this she also taught herself to think that there was a certain merit in refusing herself the natural delight of a lover, even though the possession of the lover were compatible with all her duties to herself, her father and mother, and the world at large. It was not that she had determined to have no lover. She made no such resolve, and when the proper lover came he was admitted to her heart. But she declared to herself unconsciously that she must put a guard upon herself, lest she should be betrayed into weakness by her own happiness. She had resolved that in loving her lord she would not worship him, and that in giving her heart she would only so give it as it should be given to a human creature like herself. She had acted on these high resolves, and hence it had come to pass, – not unnaturally, – that Mr. Godfrey Holmes had told her that it was 'her fault.'

She was a pretty, fair girl, with soft dark-brown hair, and soft long dark eyelashes. Her grey eyes, though quiet in their tone, were tender and lustrous. Her face was oval, and the lines of her cheek and chin perfect in their symmetry. She was generally quiet in her demeanour, but when moved she could rouse herself to great energy, and speak with feeling and almost with fire. Her fault was a reverence for martyrdom in general, and a feeling, of which she was unconscious, that it became a young woman to be unhappy in secret; – that it became a young woman I might rather say, to have a source of unhappiness hidden from the world in general, and endured without any detriment to her outward cheerfulness. We know the story of the Spartan boy who held the fox under his tunic. The fox was biting into him, – into the very entrails; but the young hero spake never a word. Now Bessy Garrow was inclined to think that it was a good thing to have a fox always biting, so that the torment caused no ruffling to her outward smiles. Now at this moment the fox within her bosom was biting her sore enough, but she bore it without flinching.

'If you would rather that he should not come I will have it arranged,' her mother had said to her.

'Not for worlds,' she had answered. 'I should never think well of myself again.'

Her mother had changed her own mind more than once as to the conduct in this matter which might be best for her to follow, thinking solely of her daughter's welfare. 'If he comes they will be reconciled, and she will be happy,' had been her first idea. But then there was a stern fixedness of purpose in Bessy's words when she spoke of Mr. Holmes, which had expelled this hope, and Mrs. Garrow had for a while thought it better that the young man should not come. But Bessy would not permit this. It would vex her father, put out of course the arrangements of other people, and display weakness on her own part. He should come, and she would endure without flinching while the fox gnawed at her.

That battle of the mistletoe had been fought on the morning before Christmas-day, and the Holmes's came on Christmas-eve. Isabella was comparatively a stranger, and therefore received at first the greater share of attention. She and Elizabeth had once seen each other, and for the last year or two had corresponded, but personally they had never been intimate. Unfortunately for the latter, that story of Godfrey's offer and acceptance had been communicated to Isabella, as had of course the immediately subsequent story of the separation. But now it would be almost impossible to avoid the subject in conversation. 'Dearest Isabella, let it be as though it had never been,' she had said in one of her letters. But sometimes it is very difficult to let things be as though they had never been.

The first evening passed over very well. The two Coverdale girls were there, and there had been much talking and merry laughter, rather juvenile in its nature, but on the whole none the worse for that. Isabella Holmes was a fine, tall, handsome girl; good-humoured, and well disposed to be pleased; rather Frenchified in her manners, and quite able to take care of herself. But she was not above round games, and did not turn up her nose at the boys. Godfrey behaved himself excellently, talking much to the Major, but by no means avoiding Miss Garrow. Mrs. Garrow, though she had known him since he was a boy, had taken an aversion to him since he had quarrelled with her daughter; but there was no room on this first night for showing such aversion, and everything went off well.

'Godfrey is very much improved,' the Major said to his wife that night.

'Do you think so?'

'Indeed I do. He has filled out and become a fine man.'

'In personal appearance, you mean. Yes, he is well-looking enough.'

'And in his manner too. He is doing uncommonly well in Liverpool, I can tell you; and if he should think of Bessy –'

'There is nothing of that sort,' said Mrs. Garrow.

'He did speak to me, you know, – two years ago. Bessy was too young then, and so indeed was he. But if she likes him –'

'I don't think she does.'

'Then there's an end of it.' And so they went to bed.

'Frank,' said the sister to her elder brother, knocking at his door when they had all gone up stairs, 'may I come in, – if you are not in bed?'

'In bed,' said he, looking up with some little pride from his Greek book; 'I've one hundred and fifty lines to do before I can get to bed. It'll be two, I suppose. I've got to mug uncommon hard these holidays. I have only one more half, you know, and then –'

'Don't overdo it, Frank.'

'No; I won't overdo it. I mean to take one day a week, and work eight hours a day on the other five. That will be forty hours a week, and will give me just two hundred hours for the holidays. I have got it all down here on a table. That will be a hundred and five for Greek play, forty for Algebra –' and so he explained to her the exact destiny of all his long hours of proposed labour. He had as yet been home a day and a half, and had succeeded in drawing out with red lines and blue figures the table which he showed her. 'If I can do that, it will be pretty well; won't it?'

'But, Frank, you have come home for your holidays, – to enjoy yourself?'

'But a fellow must work now-a-days.'

'Don't overdo it, dear; that's all. But, Frank, I could not rest if I went to bed without speaking to you. You made me unhappy today.'

'Did I, Bessy?'

'You called me a Puritan, and then you quoted that ill-natured French proverb at me. Do you really believe your sister thinks evil, Frank?' and as she spoke she put her arm caressingly round his neck.

'Of course I don't.'

'Then why say so? Harry is so much younger and so thoughtless that I can bear what he says without so much suffering. But if you and I are not friends I shall be very wretched. If you knew how I have looked forward to your coming home!'

'I did not mean to vex you, and I won't say such things again.'

'That's my own Frank. What I said to mamma, I said because I thought it right; but you must not say that I am a Puritan. I would do anything in my power to make your holidays bright and pleasant. I know that boys require so much more to amuse them than girls do. Good night, dearest; pray don't over-do yourself with work, and do take care of your eyes.' So saying she kissed him and went her way. In twenty minutes after that, he had gone to sleep over his book; and when he woke up to find the candle guttering down, he resolved that he would not begin his measured hours till Christmas-day was fairly over.

The morning of Christmas-day passed very quietly. They all went to church, and then sat round the fire chatting until the four-o'clock dinner was ready. The Coverdale girls thought it was rather more dull than former Thwaite Hall festivities, and Frank was seen to yawn. But then everybody knows that the real fun of Christmas never begins till the day itself be passed. The beef and pudding are ponderous, and unless there be absolute children in the party, there is a difficulty in grafting any special afternoon amusements on the Sunday pursuits of the morning. In the evening they were to have a dance; – that had been distinctly promised to Patty Coverdale; but the dance would not commence till eight. The beef and pudding were ponderous, but with due efforts they were overcome and disappeared. The glass of port was sipped, the almonds and raisins were nibbled, and then the ladies left the room. Ten minutes after that Elizabeth found herself seated with Isabella Holmes over the fire in her father's little book-room. It was not by her that this meeting was arranged, for she dreaded such a constrained confidence; but of course it could not be avoided, and perhaps it might be as well now as hereafter.

'Bessy,' said the elder girl, 'I am dying to be alone with you for a moment.'

'Well, you shall not die; that is, if being alone with me will save you.'

'I have so much to say to you. And if you have any true friendship in you, you also will have so much to say to me.' Miss Garrow perhaps had no true friendship in her at that moment for she would gladly have avoided saying anything, had that been possible. But, in order to prove that she was not deficient in friendship, she gave her friend her hand.

'And now tell me everything about Godfrey,' said Isabella.

'Dear Bella, I have nothing to tell, – literally nothing.'

'That is nonsense. Stop a moment, dear, and understand that I do not mean to offend you. It cannot be that you have nothing to tell, if you choose to tell it. You are not the girl to have accepted Godfrey without loving him, nor is he the man to have asked you without loving you. When you write me word that you have changed your mind, as you might about a dress, of course I know you have not told me all. Now I insist upon knowing it, – that is, if we are to be friends. I would not speak a word to Godfrey till I had seen you, in order that I might hear your story first.'

'Indeed, Bella, there is no story to tell.'

'Then I must ask him.'

'If you wish to play the part of a true friend to me, you will let the matter pass by and say nothing. You must understand that, circumstanced as we are, your brother's visit here, – what I mean is, that it is very difficult for me to act and speak exactly as I should do, and a few unfortunate words spoken may make my position unendurable.'

'Will you answer me one question!'

'I cannot tell. I think I will.'

'Do you love him?' For a moment or two Bessy remained silent, striving to arrange her words so that they should contain no falsehood, and yet betray no truth. 'Ah, I see you do,' continued Miss Holmes. 'But of course you do. Why else did you accept him?'

'I fancied that I did, as young ladies do sometimes fancy.'

'And will you say that you do not, now?' Again Bessy was silent, and then her friend rose from her seat. 'I see it all,' she said. 'What a pity it was that you both had not some friend like me by you at the time! But perhaps it may not be too late.'

I need not repeat at length all the protestations which upon this were poured forth with hot energy by poor Bessy. She endeavoured to explain how great had been the difficulty of her position. This Christmas visit had been arranged before that unhappy affair at Liverpool had occurred. Isabella's visit had been partly one of business, it being necessary that certain money affairs should be arranged between her, her brother, and the Major. 'I determined,' said Bessy, 'not to let my feelings stand in the way; and hoped that things might settle down to their former friendly footing. I already fear that I have been wrong, but it will be ungenerous in you to punish me.' Then she went on to say that if anybody attempted to interfere with her, she should at once go away to her mother's sister, who lived at Hexham, in Northumberland.

Then came the dance, and the hearts of Kate and Patty Coverdale were at last happy. But here again poor Bessy was made to understand how terribly difficult was this experiment of entertaining on a footing of friendship a lover with whom she had quarrelled only a month or two before. That she must as a necessity become the partner of Godfrey Holmes she had already calculated, and so much she was prepared to endure.

Her brothers would of course dance with the Coverdale girls, and her father would of course stand up with Isabella. There was no other possible arrangement, at any rate as a beginning. She had schooled herself too as to the way in which she would speak to him on the occasion, and how she would remain mistress of herself and of her thoughts. But when the time came the difficulty was almost too much for her.

'You do not care much for dancing, if I remember?' said he.

'Oh yes, I do. Not as Patty Coverdale does. It's a passion with her. But then I am older than Patty Coverdale.' After that he was silent for a minute or two.

'It seems so odd for me to be here again,' he said. It was odd; – she felt that it was odd. But he ought not to have said so.

'Two years make a great difference. The boys have grown so much.'

'Yes, and there are other things,' said he.

'Bella was never here before; at least not with you.'

'No. But I did not exactly mean that. All that would not make the place so strange. But your mother seems altered to me. She used to be almost like my own mother.'

'I suppose she finds that you are a more formidable person as you grow older. It was all very well scolding you when you were a clerk in the bank, but it does not do to scold the manager. These are the penalties men pay for becoming great.'

'It is not my greatness that stands in my way, but –'

'Then I'm sure I cannot say what it is. But Patty will scold you if you do not mind the figure, though you were the whole Board of Directors packed into one. She won't respect you if you neglect your present work.'

When Bessy went to bed that night she began to feel that she had attempted too much. 'Mamma,' she said, 'could I not make some excuse and go away to Aunt Mary?'

'What, now?'

'Yes, mamma; now; tomorrow. I need not say that it will make me very unhappy to be away at such a time, but I begin to think that it will be better.'

'What will papa say?'

'You must tell him all.'

'And Aunt Mary must be told also. You would not like that. Has he said anything?'

'No, nothing; – very little, that is. But Bella has spoken to me. Oh, mamma, I think we have been very wrong in this. That is, I have been wrong. I feel as though I should disgrace myself, and turn the whole party here into a misfortune.'

It would be dreadful, that telling of the story to her father and to her aunt, and such a necessity must, if possible, be avoided. Should such a necessity actually come, the former task would, no doubt, be done by her mother, but that would not lighten the load materially. After a fortnight she would again meet her father, and would be forced to discuss it. 'I will remain if it be possible,' she said; 'but, mamma, if I wish to go, you will not stop me?' Her mother promised that she would not stop her, but strongly advised her to stand her ground.

On the following morning, when she came down stairs before breakfast, she found Frank standing in the hall with his gun of which he was trying the lock. 'It is not loaded, is it, Frank?' said she.

'Oh dear, no; no one thinks of loading now-a-days till he has got out of the house. Directly after breakfast I am going across with Godfrey to the back of Greystock, to see after some moor-fowl. He asked me to go, and I couldn't well refuse.'

'Of course not. Why should you?'

'It will be deuced hard work to make up the time. I was to have been up at four this morning, but that alarum went off and never woke me. However, I shall be able to do something to-night.'

'Don't make a slavery of your holidays, Frank. What's the good of having a new gun if you're not to use it?'

'It's not the new gun. I'm not such a child as that comes to. But, you see, Godfrey is here, and one ought to be civil to him. I'll tell you what I want you girls to do, Bessy. You must come and meet us on our way home. Come over in the boat and along the path to the Patterdale road. We'll be there under the hill at about five.'

'And if you are not, we are to wait in the snow?'

'Don't make difficulties, Bessy. I tell you we will be there. We are to go in the cart, and so shall have plenty of time.'

'And how do you know the other girls will go?'

'Why, to tell you the truth, Patty Coverdale has promised. As for Miss Holmes, if she won't, why you must leave her at home with mamma. But Kate and Patty can't come without you.'

'Your discretion has found that out, has it?'

'They say so. But you will come; won't you Bessy? As for waiting, it's all nonsense. Of course you can walk on. But we'll be at the stile by five. I've got my watch, you know.' And then Bessy promised him. What would she not have done for him that was in her power to do?

'Go! Of course I'll go,' said Miss Holmes. 'I'm up to anything. I'd have gone with them this morning, and have taken a gun if they'd asked me. But, by the bye, I'd better not.'

'Why not? said Patty, who was hardly yet without fear lest something should mar the expedition.

'What will three gentlemen do with four ladies?'

'Oh, I forgot,' said Patty innocently.

'I'm sure I don't care,' said Kate; 'you may have Harry if you like.'

'Thank you for nothing,' said Miss Holmes. 'I want one for myself. It's all very well for you to make the offer, but what should I do if Harry wouldn't have me? There are two sides, you know, to every bargain.'

'I'm sure he isn't anything to me,' said Kate. 'Why, he's not quite seventeen years old yet!'

'Poor boy! What a shame to dispose of him so soon. We'll let him off for a year or two; won't we, Miss Coverdale? But as there seems by acknowledgment to be one beau with unappropriated services –'

'I'm sure I have appropriated nobody,' said Patty, 'and didn't intend.'

'Godfrey, then, is the only knight whose services are claimed,' said Miss Holmes, looking at Bessy. Bessy made no immediate answer with either her eyes or tongue; but when the Coverdales were gone, she took her new friend to task.

'How can you fill those young girls' heads with such nonsense?'

'Nature has done that, my dear.'

'But nature should be trained; should it not? You will make them think that those foolish boys are in love with them.'

'The foolish boys, as you call them, will look after that themselves. It seems to me that the foolish boys know what they are about better than some of their elders.' And then, after a moment's pause, she added, 'As for my brother, I have no patience with him.'

'Pray do not discuss your brother,' said Bessy. 'And, Bella, unless you wish to drive me away, pray do not speak of him and me together as you did just now.'

'Are you so bad as that, – that the slightest commonplace joke upsets you? Would not his services be due to you as a matter of course? If you are so sore about it, you will betray your own secret.'

'I have no secret, – none at least from you, or from mamma; and, indeed, none from him. We were both very foolish, thinking that we knew each other and our own hearts, when we knew neither.'

'I hate to hear people talk of knowing their hearts. My idea is, that if you like a young man, and he asks you to marry him, you ought to have him. That is, if there is enough to live on. I don't know what more is wanted. But girls are getting to talk and think as though they were to send their hearts through some fiery furnace of trial before they may give them up to a husband's keeping. I'm not at all sure that the French fashion is not the best, and that these things shouldn't be managed by the fathers and mothers, or perhaps by the family lawyers. Girls who are so intent upon knowing their own hearts generally end by knowing nobody's heart but their own; and then they die old maids.'

'Better that than give themselves to the keeping of those they don't know and cannot esteem.'

'That's a matter of taste. I mean to take the first that comes, so long as he looks like a gentleman, and has not less than eight hundred a year. Now Godfrey does look like a gentleman, and has double that. If I had such a chance I shouldn't think twice about it.'

'But I have no such chance. And if you have not, you would not think of it at all.'

'That's the way the wind blows; is it?'

'No, no. Oh, Bella, pray, pray leave me alone. Pray do not interfere. There is no wind blowing in any way. All that I want is your silence and your sympathy.'

'Very well. I will be silent and sympathetic as the grave. Only don't imagine that I am cold as the grave also. I don't exactly appreciate your ideas; but if I can do no good, I will at any rate endeavour to do no harm.'

After lunch, at about three, they started on their walk, and managed to ferry themselves over the river. 'Oh, do let me, Bessy,' said Kate Coverdale. 'I understand all about it. Look here, Miss Holmes. You pull the chain through your hands –'

'And inevitably tear your gloves to pieces,' said Miss Holmes. Kate certainly had done so, and did not seem to be particularly well pleased with the accident. 'There's a nasty nail in the chain,' she said. 'I wonder those stupid boys did not tell us.'

Of course they reached the trysting-place much too soon, and were very tired of walking up and down to keep their feet warm, before the sportsmen came up. But this was their own fault, seeing that they had reached the stile half an hour before the time fixed.

'I never will go anywhere to meet gentlemen again,' said Miss Holmes. 'It is most preposterous that ladies should be left in the snow for an hour. Well, young men, what sport have you had?'

'I shot the big black cock,' said Harry.

'Did you indeed?' said Kate Coverdale.

'And here are the feathers out of his tail for you. He dropped them in the water, and I had to go in after them up to my middle. But I told you that I would, so I was determined to get them.'

'Oh you silly, silly boy,' said Kate. 'But I'll keep them for ever. I will indeed.' This was said a little apart, for Harry had managed to draw the young lady aside before he presented the feathers.

Frank had also his trophies for Patty, and the tale to tell of his own prowess. In that he was a year older than his brother, he was by a year's growth less ready to tender his present to his lady-love, openly in the presence of them all. But he found his opportunity, and then he and Patty went on a little in advance. Kate also was deep in her consolations to Harry for his ducking; and therefore the four disposed of themselves in the manner previously suggested by Miss Holmes. Miss Holmes, therefore, and her brother, and Bessy Garrow, were left together in the path, and discussed the performances of the day in a manner that elicited no very ecstatic interest. So they walked for a mile, and by degrees the conversation between them dwindled down almost to nothing.

'There is nothing I dislike so much as coming out with people younger than myself,' said Miss Holmes. 'One always feels so old and dull. Listen to those children there; they make me feel as though I were an old maiden aunt, brought out with them to do propriety.'

'Patty won't at all approve if she hears you call her a child.'

'Nor shall I approve, if she treats me like an old woman,' and then she stepped on and joined the children. 'I wouldn't spoil even their sport if I could help it,' she said to herself. 'But with them I shall only be a temporary nuisance; if I remain behind I shall become a permanent evil.' And thus Bessy and her old lover were left by themselves.

'I hope you will get on well with Bella,' said Godfrey, when they had remained silent for a minute or two.

'Oh, yes. She is so good-natured and light-spirited that everybody must like her. She has been used to so much amusement and active life, that I know she must find it very dull here.'

'She is never dull anywhere, – even at Liverpool, which, for a young lady, I sometimes think the dullest place on earth. I know it is for a man.'

'A man who has work to do can never be dull; can he?'

'Indeed he can; as dull as death. I am so often enough. I have never been very bright there, Bessy, since you left us.' There was nothing in his calling her Bessy, for it had become a habit with him since they were children; and they had formerly agreed that everything between them should be as it had been before that foolish whisper of love had been spoken and received. Indeed, provision had been made by them specially on this point, so that there need be no awkwardness in this mode of addressing each other. Such provision had seemed to be very prudent, but it hardly had the desired effect on the present occasion.

'I hardly know what you mean by brightness,' she said, after a pause. 'Perhaps it is not intended that people's lives should be what you call bright.'

'Life ought to be as bright as we can make it.'

'It all depends on the meaning of the word. I suppose we are not very bright here at Thwaite Hall, but yet we think ourselves very happy.'

'I am sure you are,' said Godfrey. 'I very often think of you here.'

'We always think of places where we have been when we were young,' said Bessy; and then again they walked on for some way in silence, and Bessy began to increase her pace with the view of catching the children. The present walk to her was anything but bright, and she bethought herself with dismay that there were still two miles before she reached the Ferry.

'Bessy,' Godfrey said at last. And then he stopped as though he were doubtful how to proceed. She, however, did not say a word, but walked on quickly, as though her only hope was in catching the party before her. But they also were walking quickly, for Bella had determined that she would not be caught.

'Bessy, I must speak to you once of what passed between us at Liverpool.'

'Must you?' said she.

'Unless you positively forbid it.'

'Stop, Godfrey,' she said. And they did stop in the path, for now she no longer thought of putting an end to her embarrassment by overtaking her companions. 'If any such words are necessary for your comfort, it would hardly become me to forbid them. Were I to speak so harshly you would accuse me afterwards in your own heart. It must be for you to judge whether it is well to re-open a wound that is nearly healed.'

'But with me it is not nearly healed. The wound is open always.'

'There are some hurts,' she said, 'which do not admit of an absolute and perfect cure, unless after long years.' As she said so, she could not but think how much better was his chance of such perfect cure than her own. With her, – so she said to herself, – such curing was all but impossible; whereas with him, it was as impossible that the injury should last.

'Bessy,' he said, and he again stopped her on the narrow path, standing immediately before her on the way, 'you remember all the circumstances that made us part?'

'Yes; I think I remember them.'

'And you still think that we were right to part?'

She paused for a moment before she answered him; but it was only for a moment, and then she spoke quite firmly. 'Yes, Godfrey, I do; I have thought about it much since then. I have thought, I fear, to no good purpose about aught else. But I have never thought that we had been unwise in that.'

'And yet I think you loved me.'

'I am bound to confess I did so, as otherwise I must confess myself a liar. I told you at the time that I loved you, and I told you so truly. But it is better, ten times better, that those who love should part, even though they still should love, than that two should be joined together who are incapable of making each other happy. Remember what you told me.'

'I do remember.'

'You found yourself unhappy in your engagement, and you said it was my fault.'

'Bessy, there is my hand. If you have ceased to love me, there is an end of it. But if you love me still, let all that be forgotten.'

'Forgotten, Godfrey! How can it be forgotten? You were unhappy, and it was my fault. My fault, as it would be if I tried to solace a sick child with arithmetic, or feed a dog with grass. I had no right to love you, knowing you as I did; and knowing also that my ways would not be your ways. My punishment I understand, and it is not more than I can bear; but I had hoped that your punishment would have been soon over.'

'You are too proud, Bessy.'

'That is very likely. Frank says that I am a Puritan, and pride was the worst of their sins.'

'Too proud and unbending. In marriage should not the man and woman adapt themselves to each other?'

'When they are married, yes. And every girl who thinks of marrying should know that in very much she must adapt herself to her husband. But I do not think that a woman should be the ivy, to take the direction of every branch of the tree to which she clings. If she does so, what can be her own character? But we must go on, or we shall be too late.'

'And you will give me no other answer?'

'None other, Godfrey. Have you not just now, at this very moment, told me that I was too proud? Can it be possible that you should wish to tie yourself for life to female pride? And if you tell me that now, at such a moment as this, what would you tell me in the close intimacy of married life, when the trifles of every day would have worn away the courtesies of guest and lover?'

There was a sharpness of rebuke in this which Godfrey Holmes could not at the moment overcome. Nevertheless he knew the girl, and understood the workings of her heart and mind. Now, in her present state, she could be unbending, proud, and almost rough. In that she had much to lose in declining the renewed offer which he made her, she would, as it were, continually prompt herself to be harsh and inflexible. Had he been poor, had she not loved him, had not all good things seemed to have attended the promise of such a marriage, she would have been less suspicious of herself in receiving the offer, and more gracious in replying to it. Had he lost all his money before he came back to her, she would have taken him at once; or had he been deprived of an eye, or become crippled in his legs, she would have done so. But, circumstanced as he was, she had no motive to tenderness. There was an organic defect in her character, which no doubt was plainly marked by its own bump in her cranium, – the bump of philomartyrdom, it might properly be called. She had shipwrecked her own happiness in rejecting Godfrey Holmes; but it seemed to her to be the proper thing that a well-behaved young lady should shipwreck her own happiness. For the last month or two she had been tossed about by the waters and was nearly drowned. Now there was beautiful land again close to her, and a strong pleasant hand stretched out to save her. But though she had suffered terribly among the waves, she still thought it wrong to be saved. It would be so pleasant to take that hand, so sweet, so joyous, that it surely must be wrong. That was her doctrine; and Godfrey Holmes, though he hardly analyzed the matter, partly understood that it was so. And yet, if once she were landed on that green island, she would be so happy. She spoke with scorn of a woman clinging to a tree like ivy; and yet, were she once married, no woman would cling to her husband with sweeter feminine tenacity than Bessy Garrow. He spoke no further word to her as he walked home, but in handing her down to the ferry-boat he pressed her hand. For a second it seemed as though she had returned this pressure. If so, the action was involuntary, and her hand instantly resumed its stiffness to his touch.

It was late that night when Major Garrow went to his bed-room, but his wife was still up, waiting for him. 'Well,' said she, 'what has he said to you? He has been with you above an hour.'

'Such stories are not very quickly told; and in this case it was necessary to understand him very accurately. At length I think I do understand him.'

It is not necessary to repeat at length all that was said on that night between Major and Mrs. Garrow, as to the offer which had now for a third time been made to their daughter. On that evening after the ladies had gone, and when the two boys had taken themselves off, Godfrey Holmes told his tale to his host, and had honestly explained to him what he believed to be the state of his daughter's feelings. 'Now you know all,' said he. 'I do believe that she loves me, and if she does, perhaps she may still listen to you.' Major Garrow did not feel sure that he 'knew it all.' But when he had fully discussed the matter that night with his wife, then he thought that perhaps he had arrived at that knowledge.

On the following morning Bessy learned from the maid, at an early hour, that Godfrey Holmes had left Thwaite Hall and gone back to Liverpool. To the girl she said nothing on the subject, but she felt obliged to say a word or two to Bella. 'It is his coming that I regret,' she said; – 'that he should have had the trouble and annoyance for nothing. I acknowledge that it was my fault, and I am very sorry.'

'It cannot be helped,' said Miss Holmes, somewhat gravely. 'As to his misfortunes, I presume that his journeys between here and Liverpool are not the worst of them.'

After breakfast on that day Bessy was summoned into her

father's book-room, and found him there, and her mother also. 'Bessy,' said he, 'sit down, my dear. You know why Godfrey has left us this morning?'

Bessy walked round the room, so that in sitting she might be close to her mother and take her mother's hand in her own. 'I suppose I do, papa,' she said.

'He was with me late last night, Bessy; and when he told me what had passed between you I agreed with him that he had better go.'

'It was better that he should go, papa.'

'But he has left a message for you.'

'A message, papa?'

'Yes, Bessy. And your mother agrees with me that it had better be given to you. It is this, – that if you will send him word to come again, he will be here by Twelfth-night. He came before on my invitation, but if he returns it must be on yours.'

'Oh, papa, I cannot.'

'I do not say that you can, but think of it calmly before you altogether refuse. You shall give me your answer on New Year's morning.'

'Mamma knows that it would be impossible,' said Bessy.

'Not impossible, dearest.'

'In such a matter you should do what you believe to be right,' said her father.

'If I were to ask him here again, it would be telling him that I would –'

'Exactly, Bessy. It would be telling him that you would be his wife. He would understand it so, and so would your mother and I. It must be so understood altogether.'

'But, papa, when we were at Liverpool –'

'I have told him everything, dearest,' said Mrs. Garrow.

'I think I understand the whole,' said the Major; 'and in such a matter as this I will not give you counsel on either side. But you must remember that in making up your mind, you must think of him as well as of yourself. If you do not love him; – if you feel that as his wife you should not love him, there is not another word to be said. I need not explain to my daughter that under such circumstances she would be wrong to encourage the visits of a suitor. But your mother says you do love him.'

'Oh, mamma!'

'I will not ask you. But if you do; – if you have so told him, and allowed him to build up an idea of his life-happiness on such telling, you will, I think, sin greatly against him by allowing a false feminine pride to mar his happiness. When once a girl has confessed to a man that she loves him, the confession and the love together put upon her the burden of a duty towards him, which she cannot with impunity throw aside.' Then he kissed her, and bidding her give him a reply on the morning of the new year, left her with her mother.

She had four days for consideration, and they went past her by no means easily. Could she have been alone with her mother, the struggle would not have been so painful; but there was the necessity that she should talk to Isabella Holmes, and the necessity also that she should not neglect the Coverdales. Nothing could have been kinder than Bella. She did not speak on the subject till the morning of the last day, and then only in a very few words. 'Bessy,' she said, 'as you are great, be merciful.'

'But I am not great, and it would not be mercy.'

'As to that,' said Bella 'he has surely a right to his own opinion.'

On that evening she was sitting alone in her room when her mother came to her, and her eyes were red with weeping. Pen and paper were before her, as though she were resolved to write, but hitherto no word had been written.

'Well, Bessy,' said her mother, sitting down close beside her; 'is the deed done?'

'What deed, mamma? Who says that I am to do it?'

'The deed is not the writing, but the resolution to write. Five words will be sufficient, – if only those five words may be written.'

'It is for one's whole life, mamma. For his life, as well as my own.'

'True, Bessy; – that is quite true. But equally true whether you bid him come or allow him to remain away. That task of making up one's mind for life, must at last be done in some special moment of that life.'

'Mamma, mamma; tell me what I should do.'

But this Mrs. Garrow would not do. 'I will write the words for you if you like,' she said, 'but it is you who must resolve that they shall be written. I cannot bid my darling go away and leave me for another home; – I can only say that in my heart I do believe that home would be a happy one.'

It was morning before the note was written, but when the morning came Bessy had written it and brought it to her mother. 'You must take it to papa,' she said. Then she went and hid herself from all eyes till the noon had passed. 'Dear Godfrey,' the letter ran, 'Papa says that you will return on Wednesday if I write to ask you. Do come back to us, – if you wish it. Yours always,   BESSY.'

'It is as good as though she had filled the sheet,' said the Major. But in sending it to Godfrey Holmes, he did not omit a few accompanying remarks of his own.

An answer came from Godfrey by return of post; and on the afternoon of the sixth of January, Frank Garrow drove over to the station at Penrith to meet him. On their way back to Thwaite Hall there grew up a very close confidence between the two future brothers-in-law, and Frank explained with great perspicuity a little plan which he had arranged himself. 'As soon as it is dark, so that he won't see it, Harry will hang it up in the dining-room,' he said, 'and mind you go in there before you go anywhere else.'

'I am very glad you have come back, Godfrey,' said the Major, meeting him in the hall.

'God bless you, dear Godfrey,' said Mrs. Garrow, 'you will find Bessy in the dining-room,' she whispered; but in so whispering she was quite unconscious of the mistletoe bough.

And so also was Bessy, nor do I think that she was much more conscious when that introduction was over. Godfrey had made all manner of promises to Frank, but when the moment arrived, he had found the moment too important for any special reference to the little bough above his head. Not so, however, Patty Coverdale. 'It's a shame,' she said, bursting out of the room, 'and if I'd known what you had done, nothing on earth should have induced me to go in. I won't enter the room till I know that you have taken it out.' Nevertheless her sister Kate was bold enough to solve the mystery before the evening was over.

THE PARSON'S DAUGHTER OF OXNEY COLNE

The prettiest scenery in all England – and if I am contradicted in that assertion, I will say in all Europe – is in Devonshire, on the southern and south-eastern skirts of Dartmoor, where the rivers Dart, and Avon, and Teign form themselves, and where the broken moor is half cultivated, and the wild-looking upland fields are half moor. In making this assertion I am often met with much doubt, but it is by persons who do not really know the locality. Men and women talk to me on the matter, who have travelled down the line of railway from Exeter to Plymouth, who have spent a fortnight at Torquay, and perhaps made an excursion from Tavistock to the convict prison on Dartmoor. But who knows the glories of Chagford? Who has walked through the parish of Manaton? Who is conversant with Lustleigh Cleeves and Withycombe in the moor? Who has explored Holne Chase? Gentle reader, believe me that you will be rash in contradicting me, unless you have done these things.

There or thereabouts – I will not say by the waters of which little river it is washed – is the parish of Oxney Colne. And for those who would wish to see all the beauties of this lovely country, a sojourn in Oxney Colne would be most desirable, seeing that the sojourner would then be brought nearer to all that he would wish to visit, than at any other spot in the country. But there is an objection to any such arrangement. There are only two decent houses in the whole parish, and these are – or were when I knew the locality – small and fully occupied by their possessors. The larger and better is the parsonage, in which lived the parson and his daughter; and the smaller is the freehold residence of a certain Miss Le Smyrger, who owned a farm of a hundred acres, which was rented by one Farmer Cloysey, and who also possessed some thirty acres round her own house, which she managed herself, regarding herself to be quite as great in cream as Mr. Cloysey, and altogether superior to him in the article of cider. 'But yeu has to pay no rent, Miss,' Farmer Cloysey would say, when Miss Le Smyrger expressed this opinion of her art in a manner too defiant. 'Yeu pays no rent, or yeu couldn't do it.' Miss Le Smyrger was an old maid, with a pedigree and blood of her own, a hundred and thirty acres of fee-simple land on the borders of Dartmoor, fifty years of age, a constitution of iron, and an opinion of her own on every subject under the sun.

And now for the parson and his daughter. The parson's name was Woolsworthy – or Woolathy as it was pronounced by all those who lived around him – the Rev. Saul Woolsworthy; and his daughter was Patience Woolsworthy, or Miss Patty, as she was known to the Devonshire world of those parts. That name of Patience had not been well chosen for her, for she was a hot-tempered damsel, warm in her convictions, and inclined to express them freely. She had but two closely intimate friends in the world, and by both of them this freedom of expression had now been fully permitted to her since she was a child. Miss Le Smyrger and her father were well accustomed to her ways, and on the whole well satisfied with them. The former was equally free and equally warm-tempered as herself, and as Mr. Woolsworthy was allowed by his daughter to be quite paramount on his own subject – for he had a subject – he did not object to his daughter being paramount on all others. A pretty girl was Patience Woolsworthy at the time of which I am writing, and one who possessed much that was worthy of remark and admiration, had she lived where beauty meets with admiration, or where force of character is remarked. But at Oxney Colne, on the borders of Dartmoor, there were few to appreciate her, and it seemed as though she herself had but little idea of carrying her talent further afield, so that it might not remain for ever wrapped in a blanket.

She was a pretty girl, tall and slender, with dark eyes and black hair. Her eyes were perhaps too round for regular beauty, and her hair was perhaps too crisp; her mouth was large and expressive; her nose was finely formed, though a critic in female form might have declared it to be somewhat broad. But her countenance altogether was wonderfully attractive – if only it might be seen without that resolution for dominion which occasionally marred it, though sometimes it even added to her attractions.

It must be confessed on behalf of Patience Woolsworthy, that the circumstances of her life had peremptorily called upon her to exercise dominion. She had lost her mother when she was sixteen, and had had neither brother nor sister. She had no neighbours near her fit either from education or rank to interfere in the conduct of her life, excepting always Miss Le Smyrger. Miss Le Smyrger would have done anything for her, including the whole management of her morals and of the parsonage household, had Patience been content with such an arrangement. But much as Patience had ever loved Miss Le Smyrger, she was not content with this, and therefore she had been called on to put forth a strong hand of her own. She had put forth this strong hand early, and hence had come the character which I am attempting to describe. But I must say on behalf of this girl, that it was not only over others that she thus exercised dominion. In acquiring that power she had also acquired the much greater power of exercising rule over herself.

But why should her father have been ignored in these family arrangements? Perhaps it may almost suffice to say, that of all living men her father was the man best conversant with the antiquities of the county in which he lived. He was the Jonathan Oldbuck of Devonshire, and especially of Dartmoor, without that decision of character which enabled Oldbuck to keep his womenkind in some kind of subjection, and probably enabled him also to see that his weekly bills did not pass their proper limits. Our Mr. Oldbuck, of Oxney Colne, was sadly deficient in these. As a parish pastor with but a small cure, he did his duty with sufficient energy to keep him, at any rate, from reproach. He was kind and charitable to the poor, punctual in his services, forbearing with the farmers around him, mild with his brother clergymen, and indifferent to aught that bishop or archdeacon might think or say of him. I do not name this latter attribute as a virtue, but as a fact. But all these points were as nothing in the known character of Mr. Woolsworthy, of Oxney Colne. He was the antiquarian of Dartmoor. That was his line of life. It was in that capacity that he was known to the Devonshire world; it was as such that he

journeyed about with his humble carpet-bag, staying away
from his parsonage a night or two at a time; it was in that
character that he received now and again stray visitors in the
single spare bedroom – not friends asked to see him and his
girl because of their friendship – but men who knew something as to this buried stone, or that old land-mark. In all these
things his daughter let him have is own way, assisting and
encouraging him. That was his line of life, and therefore she
respected it. But in all other matters she chose to be paramount at the parsonage.

Mr. Woolsworthy was a little man, who always wore,
except on Sundays, grey clothes – clothes of so light a grey
that they would hardly have been regarded as clerical in a
district less remote. He had now reached a goodly age, being
full seventy years old; but still he was wiry and active, and
shewed but few symptoms of decay. His head was bald, and
the few remaining locks that surrounded it were nearly white.
But there was a look of energy about his mouth, and a
humour in his light grey eye, which forbade those who knew
him to regard him altogether as an old man. As it was, he
could walk from Oxney Colne to Priestown, fifteen long
Devonshire miles across the moor; and he who could do that
could hardly be regarded as too old for work.

But our present story will have more to do with his
daughter than with him. A pretty girl, I have said, was
Patience Woolsworthy; and one, too, in many ways remark-
able. She had taken her outlook into life, weighing the things
which she had and those which she had not, in a manner very
unusual, and, as a rule, not always desirable for a young lady.
The things which she had not were very many. She had not
society; she had not a fortune; she had not any assurance of
future means of livelihood; she had not high hope of procur-
ing for herself a position in life by marriage; she had not that
excitement and pleasure in life which she read of in such books
as found their way down to Oxney Colne Parsonage. It
would be easy to add to the list of the things which she had
not; and this list against herself she made out with the utmost
vigour. The things which she had, or those rather which she
assured herself of having, were much more easily counted.
She had the birth and education of a lady, the strength of a

healthy woman, and a will of her own. Such was the list as she made it out for herself, and I protest that I assert no more than the truth in saying that she never added to it either beauty, wit, or talent.

I began these descriptions by saying that Oxney Colne would, of all places, be the best spot from which a tourist could visit those parts of Devonshire, but for the fact that he could obtain there none of the accommodation which tourists require. A brother antiquarian might, perhaps, in those days have done so, seeing that there was, as I have said, a spare bedroom at the parsonage. Any intimate friend of Miss Le Smyrger's might be as fortunate, for she was equally well provided at Oxney Combe, by which name her house was known. But Miss Le Smyrger was not given to extensive hospitality, and it was only to those who were bound to her, either by ties of blood or of very old friendship, that she delighted to open her doors. As her old friends were very few in number, as those few lived at a distance, and as her nearest relations were higher in the world than she was, and were said by herself to look down upon her, the visits made to Oxney Combe were few and far between.

But now, at the period of which I am writing, such a visit was about to be made. Miss Le Smyrger had a younger sister, who had inherited a property in the parish of Oxney Colne equal to that of the lady who now lived there; but this the younger sister had inherited beauty also, and she therefore, in early life, had found sundry lovers, one of whom became her husband. She had married a man even then well to do in the world, but now rich and almost mighty; a Member of Parliament, a Lord of this and that board, a man who had a house in Eaton Square, and a park in the north of England; and in this way her course of life had been very much divided from that of our Miss Le Smyrger. But the Lord of the Government board had been blessed with various children; and perhaps it was now thought expedient to look after Aunt Penelope's Devonshire acres. Aunt Penelope was empowered to leave them to whom she pleased; and though it was thought in Eaton Square that she must, as a matter of course, leave them to one of the family, nevertheless a little cousinly intercourse might make the thing more certain. I will not say that this was the sole cause for such a visit, but in these days a visit was to be made by Captain Broughton to his aunt. Now Captain John Broughton was the second son of Alfonso Broughton, of Clapham Park and Eaton Square, Member of Parliament, and Lord of the aforesaid Government Board.

'And what do you mean to do with him?' Patience Woolsworthy asked of Miss Le Smyrger when that lady walked over from the Combe to say that her nephew John was to arrive on the following morning.

'Do with him? Why, I shall bring him over here to talk to your father.'

'He'll be too fashionable for that, and papa won't trouble his head about him if he finds that he doesn't care for Dartmoor.'

'Then he may fall in love with you, my dear.'

'Well, yes; there's that resource at any rate, and for your sake I dare say I should be more civil to him than papa. But he'll soon get tired of making love, and what you'll do then I cannot imagine.'

That Miss Woolsworthy felt no interest in the coming of the Captain I will not pretend to say. The advent of any stranger with whom she would be called on to associate must be matter of interest to her in that secluded place; and she was not so absolutely unlike other young ladies that the arrival of an unmarried young man would be the same to her as the advent of some patriarchal paterfamilias. In taking that outlook into life of which I have spoken she had never said to herself that she despised those things from which other girls received the excitement, the joys, and the disappointment of their lives. She had simply given herself to understand that very little of such things would come her way, and that it behoved her to live – to live happily if such might be possible – without experiencing the need of them. She had heard, when there was no thought of any such visit to Oxney Colne, that John Broughton was a handsome, clever man – one who thought much of himself, and was thought much of by others – that there had been some talk of his marrying a great heiress, which marriage, however, had not taken place through unwillingness on his part, and that he was on the whole a man of more mark in the world than the ordinary captain of ordinary regiments.

Captain Broughton came to Oxney Combe, stayed there a fortnight, – the intended period for his projected visit having been fixed at three or four days – and then went his way. He went his way back to his London haunts, the time of the year then being the close of the Easter holydays; but as he did so he told his aunt that he should assuredly return to her in the autumn.

'And assuredly I shall be happy to see you, John – if you come with a certain purpose. If you have no such purpose, you had better remain away.'

'I shall assuredly come,' the Captain had replied, and then he had gone on his journey.

The summer passed rapidly by, and very little was said between Miss Le Smyrger and Miss Woolsworthy about Captain Broughton. In many respects – nay, I may say, as to all ordinary matters, no two women could well be more intimate with each other than they were, – and more than that, they had the courage each to talk to the other with absolute truth as to things concerning themselves – a courage in which dear friends often fail. But, nevertheless, very little was said between them about Captain John Broughton. All that was said may be here repeated.

'John says that he shall return here in August,' Miss Le Smyrger said, as Patience was sitting with her in the parlour at Oxney Combe, on the morning after that gentleman's departure.

'He told me so himself,' said Patience; and as she spoke her round dark eyes assumed a look of more than ordinary self-will. If Miss Le Smyrger had intended to carry the conversation any further, she changed her mind as she looked at her companion. Then, as I said, the summer ran by, and towards the close of the warm days of July, Miss Le Smyrger, sitting in the same chair in the same room, again took up the conversation.

'I got a letter from John this morning. He says that he shall be here on the third.'

'Does he?'

'He is very punctual to the time he named.'

'Yes; I fancy that he is a punctual man,' said Patience.

'I hope that you will be glad to see him,' said Miss Le Smyrger.

'Very glad to see him,' said Patience, with a bold clear voice; and then the conversation was again dropped, and nothing further was said till after Captain Broughton's second arrival in the parish.

Four months had then passed since his departure, and during that time Miss Woolsworthy had performed all her usual daily duties in their accustomed course. No one could discover that she had been less careful in her household matters than had been her wont, less willing to go among her poor neighbours, or less assiduous in her attentions to her father. But not the less was there a feeling in the minds of those around her that some great change had come upon her. She would sit during the long summer evenings on a certain spot outside the parsonage orchard, at the top of a small sloping field in which their solitary cow was always pastured, with a book on her knees before her, but rarely reading. There she would sit, with the beautiful view down to the winding river below her, watching the setting sun, and thinking, thinking, thinking – thinking of something of which she had never spoken. Often would Miss Le Smyrger come upon her there, and sometimes would pass by her even without a word; but never – never once did she dare to ask her of the matter of her thoughts. But she knew the matter well enough. No confession was necessary to inform her that Patience Woolsworthy was in love with John Broughton – ay, in love, to the full and entire loss of her whole heart.

On one evening she was so sitting till the July sun had fallen and hidden himself for the night, when her father came upon her as he returned from one of his rambles on the moor. 'Patty,' he said 'you are always sitting there now. Is it not late? Will you not be cold?'

'No, papa,' she said, 'I shall not be cold.'

'But won't you come to the house? I miss you when you come in so late that there's no time to say a word before we go to bed.'

She got up and followed him into the parsonage, and when they were in the sitting-room together, and the door was closed, she came up to him and kissed him. 'Papa,' she said, 'would it make you very unhappy if I were to leave you?'

'Leave me!' he said, startled by the serious and almost solemn tone of her voice. 'Do you mean for always?'

'If I were to marry, papa?'

'Oh, marry! No; that would not make me unhappy. It would make me very happy, Patty, to see you married to a man you would love – very, very happy; though my days would be desolate without you.'

'That is it, papa. What would you do if I went from you?'

'What would it matter, Patty? I should be free at any rate, from a load which often presses heavy on me now. What will you do when I shall leave you? A few more years and all will be over with me. But who is it, love? Has anybody said anything to you?'

'It was only an idea, papa. I don't often think of such a thing; but I did think of it then.' And so the subject was allowed to pass by. This had happened before the day of the second arrival had been absolutely fixed and made known to Miss Woolsworthy.

And then that second arrival took place. The reader may have understood from the words with which Miss Le Smyrger authorised her nephew to make his second visit to Oxney Combe that Miss Woolsworthy's passion was not altogether unauthorised. Captain Broughton had been told that he was not to come unless he came with a certain purpose; and having been so told, he still persisted in coming. There can be no doubt but that he well understood the purport to which his aunt alluded. 'I shall assuredly come,' he had said. And true to his word, he was now there.

Patience knew exactly the hour at which he must arrive at the station at Newton Abbot, and the time also which it would take to travel over those twelve uphill miles from the station to Oxney. It need hardly be said that she paid no visit to Miss Le Smyrger's house on that afternoon; but she might have known something of Captain Broughton's approach without going thither. His road to the Combe passed by the parsonage-gate, and had Patience sat even at her bedroom window she must have seen him. But on such a morning she would not sit at her bedroom window – she would do nothing which would force her to accuse herself of a restless longing for her lover's coming. It was for him to seek her. If he chose to do so, he knew the way to the parsonage.

Miss Le Smyrger – good, dear, honest, hearty Miss Le Smyrger, was in a fever of anxiety on behalf of her friend. It was not that she wished her nephew to marry Patience – or rather that she had entertained any such wish when he first came among them. She was not given to match-making, and moreover thought, or had thought within herself, that they of Oxney Colne could do very well without any admixture from Eaton Square. Her plan of life had been that, when old Mr. Woolsworthy was taken away from Dartmoor, Patience should live with her; and that when she also shuffled off her coil, then Patience Woolsworthy should be the maiden mistress of Oxney Combe – of Oxney Combe and Mr. Cloysey's farm – to the utter detriment of all the Broughtons. Such had been her plan before nephew John had come among them – a plan not to be spoken of till the coming of that dark day which should make Patience an orphan. But now her nephew had been there, and all was to be altered. Miss Le Smyrger's plan would have provided a companion for her old age; but that had not been her chief object. She had thought more of Patience than of herself, and now it seemed that a prospect of a higher happiness was opening for her friend.

'John,' she said, as soon as the first greetings were over, 'do you remember the last words that I said to you before you went away?' Now, for myself, I much admire Miss Le Smyrger's heartiness, but I do not think much of her discretion. It would have been better, perhaps, had she allowed things to take their course.'

'I can't say that I do,' said the Captain. At the same time the Captain did remember very well what those last words had been.

'I am so glad to see you, so delighted to see you, if – if – if –,' and then she paused, for with all her courage she hardly dared to ask her nephew whether he had come there with the express purpose of asking Miss Woolsworthy to marry him.

To tell the truth – for there is no room for mystery within the limits of this short story, – to tell, I say, at a word the plain and simple truth, Captain Broughton had already asked that question. On the day before he left Oxney Colne, he had in set terms proposed to the parson's daughter, and indeed the words, the hot and frequent words, which previously to that had fallen like sweetest honey into the ears of Patience Woolsworthy, had made it imperative on him to do so. When a man in such a place as that has talked to a girl of love day after day, must not he talk of it to some definite purpose on the day on which he leaves her? Or if he do not, must he not submit to be regarded as false, selfish, and almost fraudulent? Captain Broughton, however, had asked the question honestly and truly. He had done so honestly and truly, but in words, or, perhaps, simply with a tone, that had hardly sufficed to satisfy the proud spirit of the girl he loved. She by that time had confessed to herself that she loved him with all her heart; but she had made no such confession to him. To him she had spoken no word, granted no favour, that any lover might rightfully regard as a token of love returned. She had listened to him as he spoke, and bade him keep such sayings for the drawing-rooms of his fashionable friends. Then he had spoken out and had asked for that hand, – not, perhaps, as a suitor tremulous with hope, – but as a rich man who knows that he can command that which he desires to purchase.

'You should think more of this,' she had said to him at last. 'If you would really have me for your wife, it will not be much to you to return here again when time for thinking of it shall have passed by.' With these words she had dismissed him, and now he had again come back to Oxney Colne. But still she would not place herself at the window to look for him, nor dress herself in other than her simple morning country dress, nor omit one item of her daily work. If he wished to take her at all, he should wish to take her as she really was, in her plain country life, but he should take her also with full observance of all those privileges which maidens are allowed to claim from their lovers. He should contract no ceremonious observance because she was the daughter of a poor country parson who would come to him without a shilling, whereas he stood high in the world's books. He had asked her to give him all that she had, and that all she was ready to give, without stint. But the gift must be valued before it could be given or received. He also was to give her as much, and she would accept it as being beyond all price. But she would not allow that that which was offered to her was in any degree the more precious because of his outward worldly standing.

She would not pretend to herself that she thought he would come to her that day, and therefore she busied herself in the kitchen and about the house, giving directions to her two maids as though the afternoon would pass as all other days did pass in that household. They usually dined at four, and she rarely, in these summer months, went far from the house before that hour. At four precisely she sat down with her father, and then said that she was going up as far as Helpholme after dinner. Helpholme was a solitary farmhouse in another parish, on the border of the moor, and Mr. Woolsworthy asked her whether he should accompany her.

'Do, papa,' she said, 'if you are not too tired.' And yet she had thought how probable it might be that she should meet John Broughton on her walk. And so it was arranged; but, just as dinner was over, Mr. Woolsworthy remembered himself.

'Gracious me,' he said, 'how my memory is going. Gribbles, from Ivybridge, and old John Poulter, from Bovey, are coming to meet here by appointment. You can't put Helpholme off till tomorrow?'

Patience, however, never put off anything, and therefore at six o'clock, when her father had finished his slender modicum of toddy, she tied on her hat and went on her walk. She started forth with a quick step, and left no word to say by which route she would go. As she passed up along the little lane which led towards Oxney Combe, she would not even look to see if he was coming towards her; and when she left the road, passing over a stone stile into a little path which ran first through the upland fields, and then across the moor ground towards Helphome, she did not look back once, or listen for his coming step.

She paid her visit, remaining upwards of an hour with the old bedridden mother of the tenant of Helpholme. 'God bless you, my darling!' said the old woman as she left her; 'and send you some one to make your own path bright and happy through the world.' These words were still ringing in her ears with all their significance as she saw John Broughton waiting for her at the first stile which she had to pass after leaving the farmer's haggard.

'Patty,' he said, as he took her hand, and held it close within both his own, 'what a chase I have had after you!'

'And who asked you, Captain Broughton?' she answered smiling. 'If the journey was too much for your poor London strength, could you not have waited till tomorrow morning, when you would have found me at the parsonage?' But she did not draw her hand away from him, or in any way pretend that he had not a right to accost her as a lover.

'No, I could not wait. I am more eager to see those I love than you seem to be.'

'How do you know whom I love, or how eager I might be to see them? There is an old woman there whom I love, and I have thought nothing of this walk with the object of seeing her.' And now, slowly drawing her hand away from him, she pointed to the farmhouse which she had left.

'Patty,' he said, after a minute's pause, during which she had looked full into his face with all the force of her bright eyes; 'I have come from London today, straight down here to Oxney, and from my aunt's house close upon your footsteps after you, to ask you that one question. Do you love me?'

'What a Hercules!' she said, again laughing. 'Do you really mean that you left London only this morning? Why, you must have been five hours in a railway carriage and two in a postchaise, not to talk of the walk afterwards. You ought to take more care of yourself, Captain Broughton!'

He would have been angry with her – for he did not like to be quizzed – had she not put her hand on his arm as she spoke, and the softness of her touch had redeemed the offence of her words.

'All that have I done,' said he, 'that I may hear one word from you.'

'That any word of mine should have such potency! But let us walk on, or my father will take us for some of the standing stones of the moor. How have you found your aunt? If you only knew the cares that have sat on her dear shoulders for the last week past, in order that your high mightiness might have a sufficiency to eat and drink in these desolate half-starved regions.'

'She might have saved herself such anxiety. No one can care less for such things than I do.'

'And yet I think I have heard you boast of the cook of your club.' And then again there was silence for a minute or two.

'Patty,' said he, stopping again in the path; 'answer my question. I have a right to demand an answer. Do you love me?'

'And what if I do? What if I have been so silly as to allow your perfections to be too many for my weak heart? What then, Captain Broughton?'

'It cannot be that you love me, or you would not joke now.'

'Perhaps not, indeed,' she said. It seemed as though she were resolved not to yield an inch in her own humour. And then again they walked on.

'Patty,' he said once more, 'I shall get an answer from you tonight, – this evening; now, during this walk, or I shall return tomorrow, and never revisit this spot again.'

'Oh, Captain Broughton, how should we ever manage to live without you?'

'Very well,' he said; 'up to the end of this walk I can bear it all; – and one word spoken then will mend it all.'

During the whole of this time she felt that she was ill-using him. She knew that she loved him with all her heart; that it would nearly kill her to part with him; that she had heard his renewed offer with an ecstacy of joy. She acknowledged to herself that he was giving proof of his devotion as strong as any which a girl could receive from her lover. And yet she could hardly bring herself to say the word he longed to hear. That word once said, and then she knew that she must succumb to her love for ever! That word once said, and there would be nothing for her but to spoil him with her idolatry! That word once said, and she must continue to repeat it into his ears, till perhaps he might be tired of hearing it! And now he had threatened her, and how could she speak it after that? She certainly would not speak it unless he asked her again without such threat. And so they walked on again in silence.

'Patty,' he said. 'By the heavens above us you shall answer me. Do you love me?'

She now stood still, and almost trembled as she looked up into his face. She stood opposite to him for a moment, and then placing her two hands on his shoulders, she answered him. I do, I do, I do,' she said, 'with all my heart; with all my heart – with all my heart and strength.' And then her head fell upon his breast.

Captain Broughton was almost as much surprised as delighted by the warmth of the acknowledgment made by the eager-hearted passionate girl whom he now held within his arms. She had said it now; the words had been spoken; and there was nothing for her but to swear to him over and over again with her sweetest oaths, that those words were true – true as her soul. And very sweet was the walk down from thence to the parsonage gate. He spoke no more of the distance of the ground, or the length of his day's journey. But he stopped her at every turn that he might press her arm the closer to his own, that he might look into the brightness of her eyes, and prolong his hour of delight. There were no more gibes now on her tongue, no raillery at his London finery, no laughing comments on his coming and going. With downright honesty she told him everything: how she had loved him before her heart was warranted in such a passion; how, with much thinking, she had resolved that it would be unwise to take him at his first word, and had thought it better that he should return to London, and then think over it; how she had almost repented of her courage when she had feared, during those long summer days, that he would forget her; and how her heart had leapt for joy when her old friend had told her that he was coming.

'And yet,' said he, 'you were not glad to see me!'

'Oh, was I not glad? You cannot understand the feelings of a girl who has lived secluded as I have done. Glad is no word for the joy I felt. But it was not seeing you that I cared for so much. It was the knowledge that you were near me once again. I almost wish now that I had not seen you till to-morrow.' But as she spoke she pressed his arm, and this caress gave the lie to her last words.

'No, do not come in tonight,' she said, when she reached

the little wicket that led up to the parsonage. 'Indeed, you shall not. I could not behave myself properly if you did.'

'But I don't want you to behave properly.'

'Oh! I am to keep that for London, am I? But, nevertheless, Captain Broughton, I will not invite you either to tea or to supper tonight.'

'Surely I may shake hands with your father.'

'Not tonight – not till —. John, I may tell him, may I not? I must tell him at once.'

'Certainly,' said he.

'And then you shall see him tomorrow. Let me see – at what hour shall I bid you come?'

'To breakfast.'

'No, indeed. What on earth would your aunt do with her broiled turkey and the cold pie? I have got no cold pie for you.'

'I hate cold pie.'

'What a pity! But, John, I should be forced to have you directly after breakfast. Come down – come down at two, or three; and then I will go back with you to Aunt Penelope. I must see her tomorrow;' and so at last the matter was settled, and the happy Captain, as he left her, was hardly resisted in his attempt to press her lips to his own.

When she entered the parlour in which her father was sitting, there still were Gribbles and Poulter discussing some knotty point of Devon lore. So Patience took off her hat, and sat herself down, waiting till they should go. For full an hour she had to wait, and then Gribbles and Poulter did go. But it was not in such matters as this that Patience Woolsworthy was impatient. She could wait, and wait, and wait, curbing herself for weeks and months while the thing waited for was in her eyes good; but she could not curb her hot thoughts or her hot words when things came to be discussed which she did not think to be good.

'Papa,' she said, when Gribbles' long-drawn last word had been spoken at the door. 'Do you remember how I asked you the other day what you would say if I were to leave you?'

'Yes, surely,' he replied, looking up at her in astonishment.

'I am going to leave you now,' she said. 'Dear, dearest father, how am I to go from you?'

'Going to leave me,' said he, thinking of her visit to Helpholme, and thinking of nothing else.

Now, there had been a story about Helpholme. That bed-ridden old lady there had a stalwart son, who was now the owner of the Helpholme pastures. But though owner in fee of all those wild acres, and of the cattle which they supported, he was not much above the farmers around him, either in manners or education. He had his merits, however; for he was honest, well-to-do in the world, and modest withal. How strong love had grown up, springing from neighbourly kindness, between our Patience and his mother, it needs not here to tell; but rising from it had come another love – or an ambition which might have grown to love. The young man, after much thought, had not dared to speak to Miss Wools-worthy, but he had sent a message by Miss Le Smyrger. If there could be any hope for him, he would present himself as a suitor – on trial. He did not owe a shilling in the world, and had money by him – saved. He wouldn't ask the parson for a shilling of fortune. Such had been the tenor of his message, and Miss Le Smyrger had delivered it faithfully. 'He does not mean it,' Patience had said with her stern voice. 'Indeed he does, my dear. You may be sure he is in earnest,' Miss Le Smyrger had replied; 'and there is not an honester man in these parts.'

'Tell him,' said Patience, not attending to the latter portion of her friend's last speech, 'that it cannot be – make him understand, you know – and tell him also that the matter shall be thought of no more.' The matter had, at any rate, been spoken of no more, but the young farmer still remained a bachelor, and Helpholme still wanted a mistress. But all this came back upon the parson's mind when his daughter told him that she was about to leave him.

'Yes, dearest,' she said; and as she spoke she now knelt at his knees. 'I have been asked in marriage, and I have given myself away.'

'Well, my love, if you will be happy –'

'I hope I shall; I think I shall. But you, papa?'

'You will not be far from us.'

'Oh, yes; in London.'

'In London?'

'Captain Broughton lives in London generally.'

'And has Captain Broughton asked you to marry him?'

'Yes, papa – who else? Is he not good? Will you not love him? Oh, papa, do not say that I am wrong to love him?'

He never told her his mistake, or explained to her that he had not thought it possible that the high-placed son of the London great man should have fallen in love with his un-dowered daughter; but he embraced her, and told her, with all his enthusiasm, that he rejoiced in her joy, and would be happy in her happiness. 'My own Patty,' he said, 'I have ever known that you were too good for this life of ours here.' And then the evening wore away into the night, with many tears, but still with much happiness.

Captain Broughton, as he walked back to Oxney Combe, made up his mind that he would say nothing on the matter to his aunt till the next morning. He wanted to think over it all, and to think it over, if possible, by himself. He had taken a step in life, the most important that a man is ever called on to take, and he had to reflect whether or no he had taken it with wisdom.

'Have you seen her?' said Miss Le Smyrger, very anxiously, when he came into the drawing-room.

'Miss Woolsworthy you mean,' said he. 'Yes, I've seen her. As I found her out, I took a long walk, and happened to meet her. Do you know, aunt, I think I'll go to bed; I was up at five this morning, and have been on the move ever since.'

Miss Le Smyrger perceived that she was to hear nothing that evening, so she handed him his candlestick and allowed him to go to his room.

But Captain Broughton did not immediately retire to bed, nor when he did so was he able to sleep at once. Had this step that he had taken been a wise one? He was not a man who, in worldly matters, had allowed things to arrange themselves for him, as is the case with so many men. He had formed views for himself, and had a theory of life. Money for money's sake he had declared to himself to be bad. Money, as a concomitant to things which were in themselves good, he had declared to himself to be good also. That concomitant in this affair of his marriage, he had now missed. Well; he had made up his mind to that, and would put up with the loss. He had means of living of his own, the means not so extensive as might have been desirable. That it would be well for him to become a married man, looking merely to that state of life as opposed to his present state, he had fully resolved. On that point, therefore, there was nothing to repent. That Patty Woolsworthy was good, affectionate, clever, and beautiful he was sufficiently satisfied. It would be odd indeed if he were not so satisfied now, seeing that for the last four months he had so declared to himself daily with many inward asseverations. And yet though, he repeated, now again that he was satisfied, I do not think that he was so fully satisfied of it as he had been throughout the whole of those four months. It is sad to say so, but I fear – I fear that such was the case. When you have your plaything, how much of the anticipated pleasure vanishes, especially if it be won easily.

He had told none of his family what were his intentions in this second visit to Devonshire, and now he had to bethink himself whether they would be satisfied. What would his sister say, she who had married the Honourable Augustus Gumbleton, gold-stick-in-waiting to Her Majesty's Privy Council? Would she receive Patience with open arms, and make much of her about London? And then how far would London suit Patience, or would Patience suit London? There would be much for him to do in teaching her, and it would be well for him to set about the lesson without loss of time. So far he got that night, but when the morning came he went a step further, and began mentally to criticise her manner to himself. It had been very sweet, that warm, that full, that ready declaration of love. Yes; it had been very sweet; but – but –; when, after her little jokes, she did confess her love, had she not been a little too free for feminine excellence? A man likes to be told that he is loved, but he hardly wishes that the girl he is to marry should fling herself at his head!

Ah me! yes; it was thus he argued to himself as on that morning he went through the arrangements of his toilet. 'Then he was a brute,' you say, my pretty reader. I have never said that he was not a brute. But this I remark, that many such brutes are to be met with in the beaten paths of the world's highway. When Patience Woolsworthy had answered him coldly, bidding him go back to London and think over

his love, while it seemed from her manner that at any rate as
yet she did not care for him; while he was absent from her,
and, therefore, longing for her, the possession of her charms,
her talent and bright honesty of purpose had seemed to him a
thing most desirable. Now they were his own. They had, in
fact, been his own from the first. The heart of this country-
bred girl had fallen at the first word from his mouth. Had she
not so confessed to him? She was very nice – very nice indeed.
He loved her dearly. But had he not sold himself too cheaply?

I by no means say that he was not a brute. But whether
brute or no he was an honest man, and had no remotest
dream, either then, on that morning, or during the following
days on which such thoughts pressed more thickly on his
mind – of breaking away from his pledged word. At breakfast
on that morning he told all to Miss Le Smyrger, and that lady,
with warm and gracious intentions, confided to him her
purpose regarding her property. 'I have always regarded
Patience as my heir,' she said, 'and shall do so still.'

'Oh, indeed,' said Captain Broughton.

'But it is a great, great pleasure to me to think that she will
give back the little property to my sister's child. You will have
your mother's, and thus it will all come together again.'

'Ah!' said Captain Broughton. He had his own ideas about
property, and did not, even under existing circumstances, like
to hear that his aunt considered herself at liberty to leave the
acres away to one who was by blood quite a stranger to the
family.

'Does Patience know of this?' he asked.

'Not a word,' said Miss Le Smyrger. And then nothing
more was said upon the subject.

On that afternoon he went down and received the parson's
benediction and congratulations with a good grace. Patience
said very little on the occasion, and indeed was absent during
the greater part of the interview. The two lovers then walked
up to Oxney Combe, and there were more benedictions and
more congratulations. 'All went merry as a marriage bell,' at
any rate as far as Patience was concerned. Not a word had yet
fallen from that dear mouth, not a look had yet come over
that handsome face, which tended in any way to mar her bliss.
Her first day of acknowledged love was a day altogether

happy, and when she prayed for him as she knelt beside her bed there was no feeling in her mind that any fear need disturb her joy.

I will pass over the next three or four days very quickly, merely saying that Patience did not find them so pleasant as that first day after her engagement. There was something in her lover's manner – something which at first she could not define – which by degrees seemed to grate against her feelings. He was sufficiently affectionate, that being a matter on which she did not require much demonstration; but joined to this affection there seemed to be –; she hardly liked to suggest to herself a harsh word, but could it be possible that he was beginning to think that she was not good enough for him? And then she asked herself the question – was she good enough for him? If there were doubt about that, the match should be broken off, though she tore her own heart out in the struggle. The truth, however, was this – that he had begun that teaching which he had already found to be so necessary. Now, had any one essayed to teach Patience German or mathematics, with that young lady's free consent, I believe that she would have been found a meek scholar. But it was not probable that she would be meek when she found a self-appointed tutor teaching her manners and conduct without her consent.

So matters went on for four or five days, and on the evening of the fifth day, Captain Broughton and his aunt drank tea at the parsonage. Nothing very especial occurred; but as the parson and Miss Le Smyrger insisted on playing backgammon with devoted perseverance during the whole evening, Broughton had a good opportunity of saying a word or two about those changes in his lady-love which a life in London would require – and some word he said also – some single slight word as to the higher station in life to which he would exalt his bride. Patience bore it – for her father and Miss Le Smyrger were in the room – she bore it well, speaking no syllable of anger, and enduring, for the moment, the implied scorn of the old parsonage. Then the evening broke up, and Captain Broughton walked back to Oxney Combe with his aunt. 'Patty,' her father said to her before they went to bed, 'he seems to me to be a most excellent young man.'

'Dear papa,' she answered, kissing him. 'And terribly deep in love,' said Mr. Woolsworthy. 'Oh, I don't know about that,' she answered, as she left him with her sweetest smile. But though she could thus smile at her father's joke, she had already made up her mind that there was still something to be learned as to her promised husband before she could place herself altogether in his hands. She would ask him whether he thought himself liable to injury from this proposed marriage; and though he should deny any such thought, she would know from the manner of his denial what his true feelings were.

And he, too, on that night, during his silent walk with Miss Le Smyrger, had entertained some similar thoughts. 'I fear she is obstinate,' he said to himself, and then he had half accused her of being sullen also. 'If that be her temper, what a life of misery I have before me!'

'Have you fixed a day yet?' his aunt asked him as they came near to her house.

'No not yet: I don't know whether it will suit me to fix it before I leave.'

'Why it was but the other day you were in such a hurry.'

'Ah – yes – I have thought more about it since then.'

'I should have imagined that this would depend on what Patty thinks,' said Miss Le Smyrger, standing up for the privileges of her sex. 'It is presumed that the gentleman is always ready as soon the lady will consent.'

'Yes, in ordinary cases it is so; but when a girl is taken out of her own sphere –'

'Her own sphere! Let me caution you, Master John, not to talk to Patty about her own sphere.'

'Aunt Penelope, as Patience is to be my wife and not yours, I must claim permission to speak to her on such subjects as may seem suitable to me.' And then they parted – not in the best humour with each other.

On the following day Captain Broughton and Miss Woolsworthy did not meet till the evening. She had said, before those few ill-omened words had passed her lover's lips, that she would probably be at Miss Le Smyrger's house on the following morning. Those ill-omened words did pass her lover's lips, and then she remained at home. This did not come from sullenness, nor even from anger, but from a conviction that it would be well that she should think much before she met him again. Nor was he anxious to hurry a meeting. His thought – his base thought – was this; that she would be sure to come up to the Combe after him; but she did not come, and therefore in the evening he went down to her, and asked her to walk with him.

They went away by the path that led to Helpholme, and little was said between them till they had walked some mile together. Patience, as she went along the path, remembered almost to the letter the sweet words which had greeted her ears as she came down that way with him on the night of his arrival; but he remembered nothing of that sweetness then. Had he not made an ass of himself during these last six months? That was the thought which very much had possession of his mind.

'Patience,' he said at last, having hitherto spoken only an indifferent word now and again since they had left the parsonage, 'Patience, I hope you realise the importance of the step which you and I are about to take?'

'Of course I do,' she answered: 'what an odd question that is for you to ask!'

'Because,' said he, 'sometimes I almost doubt it. It seems to me as though you thought you could remove yourself from here to your new home with no more trouble than when you go from home up to the Combe.'

'Is that meant for a reproach, John?'

'No, not for a reproach, but for advice. Certainly not for a reproach.'

'I am glad of that.'

'But I should wish to make you think how great is the leap in the world which you are about to take.' Then again they walked on for many steps before she answered him.

'Tell me then, John,' she said, when she had sufficiently considered what words she would speak; and as she spoke a bright colour suffused her face, and her eyes flashed almost with anger. 'What leap do you mean? Do you mean a leap upwards?'

'Well, yes; I hope it will be so.'

'In one sense, certainly, it would be a leap upwards. To be the wife of the man I loved; to have the privilege of holding his happiness in my hand, to know that I was his own – that would, indeed, be a leap upwards; a leap almost to heaven, if all that were so. But if you mean upwards in any other sense –'

'I was thinking of the social scale.'

'Then, Captain Broughton, your thoughts were doing me dishonour.'

'Doing you dishonour!'

'Yes, doing me dishonour. That your father is, in the world's esteem, a greater man than mine is doubtless true enough. That you, as a man, are richer than I am as a woman, is doubtless also true. But you dishonour me, and yourself also, if these things can weigh with you now.'

'Patience, – I think you can hardly know what words you are saying to me.'

'Pardon me, but I think I do. Nothing that you can give me – no gifts of that description – can weigh aught against that which I am giving you. If you had all the wealth and rank of the greatest lord in the land, it would count as nothing in such a scale. If – as I have not doubted – if in return for my heart you have given me yours, then – then – then you have paid me fully. But when gifts such as those are going, nothing else can count even as a make-weight.'

'I do not quite understand you,' he answered, after a pause. 'I fear you are a little high-flown.' And then, while the evening was still early, they walked back to the parsonage almost without another word.

Captain Broughton at this time had only one full day more to remain at Oxney Colne. On the afternoon following that he was to go as far as Exeter, and thence return to London. Of course, it was to be expected that the wedding day would be fixed before he went, and much had been said about it during the first day or two of his engagement. Then he had pressed for an early time, and Patience, with a girl's usual diffidence, had asked for some little delay. But now nothing was said on the subject; and how was it probable that such a matter could be settled after such a conversation as that which I have related? That evening, Miss Le Smyrger asked whether the day had been fixed. 'No,' said Captain Broughton harshly; 'nothing has been fixed.' 'But it will be arranged before you go.' 'Probably not,' he said; and then the subject was dropped for the time.

'John,' she said, just before she went to bed, 'if there be anything wrong between you and Patience, I conjure you to tell me.'

'You had better ask her,' he replied. 'I can tell you nothing.'

On the following morning he was much surprised by seeing Patience on the gravel path before Miss Le Smyrger's gate immediately after breakfast. He went to the door to open it for her, and she, as she gave him her hand, told him that she came up to speak to him. There was no hesitation in her manner, nor any look of anger in her face. But there was in her gait and form, in her voice and countenance, a fixedness of purpose which he had never seen before, or at any rate had never acknowledged.

'Certainly,' said he. 'Shall I come out with you, or will you come up stairs?'

'We can sit down in the summer-house,' she said; and thither they both went.

'Captain Broughton,' she said – and she began her task the moment that they were both seated – 'You and I have engaged ourselves as man and wife, but perhaps we have been over rash.'

'How so?' said he.

'It may be – and indeed I will say more – it is the case that we have made this engagement without knowing enough of each other's character.'

'I have not thought so.'

'The time will perhaps come when you will so think, but for the sake of all that we most value, let it come before it is too late. What would be our fate – how terrible would be our misery – if such a thought should come to either of us after we have linked our lots together.'

There was a solemnity about her as she thus spoke which almost repressed him, – which for a time did prevent him from taking that tone of authority which on such a subject he would choose to adopt. But he recovered himself. 'I hardly think that this comes well from you,' he said.

'From whom else should it come? Who else can fight my battle for me; and, John, who else can fight that same battle on your behalf? I tell you this, that with your mind standing towards me as it does stand at present, you could not give me your hand at the altar with true words and a happy conscience. Am I not true? You have half repented of your bargain already. Is it not so?'

He did not answer her; but getting up from his seat walked to the front of the summer-house, and stood there with his back turned upon her. It was not that he meant to be ungracious, but in truth he did not know how to answer her. He had half repented of his bargain.

'John,' she said, getting up and following him, so that she could put her hand upon his arm, 'I have been very angry with you.'

'Angry with me!' he said, turning sharp upon her.

'Yes, angry with you. You would have treated me like a child. But that feeling has gone now. I am not angry now. There is my hand; – the hand of a friend. Let the words that have been spoken between us be as though they had not been spoken. Let us both be free.'

'Do you mean it?' he asked.

'Certainly I mean it.' As she spoke these words her eyes were filled with tears, in spite of all the efforts she could make; but he was not looking at her, and her efforts had sufficed to prevent any sob from being audible.

'With all my heart,' he said; and it was manifest from his tone that he had no thought of her happiness as he spoke. It was true that she had been angry with him – angry, as she had herself declared; but nevertheless, in what she had said and what she had done, she had thought more of his happiness than of her own. Now she was angry once again.

'With all your heart, Captain Broughton! Well, so be it. If with all your heart, then is the necessity so much the greater. You go tomorrow. Shall we say farewell now?'

'Patience, I am not going to be lectured.'

'Certainly not by me. Shall we say farewell now?'

'Yes, if you are determined.'

'I am determined. Farewell, Captain Broughton. You have all my wishes for your happiness.' And she held out her hand to him.

'Patience!' he said. And he looked at her with a dark frown, as though he would strive to frighten her into submission. If so, he might have saved himself any such attempt.

'Farewell, Captain Broughton. Give me your hand, for I cannot stay.' He gave her his hand, hardly knowing why he did so. She lifted it to her lips and kissed it, and then, leaving him, passed from the summer-house down through the wicket-gate, and straight home to the parsonage.

During the whole of that day she said no word to anyone of what had occurred. When she was once more at home she went about her household affairs as she had done on that day of his arrival. When she sat down to dinner with her father he observed nothing to make him think that she was unhappy; nor during the evening was there any expression in her face, or any tone in her voice, which excited his attention. On the following morning Captain Broughton called at the parsonage, and the servant-girl brought word to her mistress that he was in the parlour. But she would not see him. 'Laws, miss, you ain't a quarrelled with your beau?' the poor girl said. 'No, not quarrelled,' she said; 'but give him that.' It was a scrap of paper, containing a word or two in pencil. 'It is better that we should not meet again. God bless you.' And from that day to this, now more than ten years, they never have met.

'Papa,' she said to her father that afternoon, 'dear papa, do not be angry with me. It is all over between me and John Broughton. Dearest, you and I will not be separated.'

It would be useless here to tell how great was the old man's surprise and how true his sorrow. As the tale was told to him no cause was given for anger with anyone. Not a word was spoken against the suitor who had on that day returned to London with a full conviction that now at least he was relieved from his engagement. 'Patty, my darling child,' he said, 'may God grant that it be for the best!'

'It is for the best,' she answered stoutly. 'For this place I am fit; and I much doubt whether I am fit for any other.'

On that day she did not see Miss Le Smyrger, but on the following morning, knowing that Captain Broughton had gone off, having heard the wheels of the carriage as they passed by the parsonage gate on his way to the station, – she walked up to the Combe.

'He has told you, I suppose?' said she.

'Yes,' said Miss Le Smyrger. 'And I will never see him again unless he asks your pardon on his knees. I have told him so. I would not even give him my hand as he went.'

'But why so, thou kindest one? The fault was mine more than his.'

'I understand. I have eyes in my head,' said the old maid. 'I have watched him for the last four or five days. If you could have kept the truth to yourself and bade him keep off from you, he would have been at your feet now, licking the dust from your shoes.'

'But, dear friend, I do not want a man to lick dust from my shoes.'

'Ah, you are a fool. You do not know the value of your own wealth.'

'True; I have been a fool. I was a fool to think that one coming from such a life as he has led could be happy with such as I am. I know the truth now. I have bought the lesson dearly, – but perhaps not too dearly, seeing that it will never be forgotten.'

There was but little more said about the matter between our three friends at Oxney Colne. What, indeed, could be said? Miss Le Smyrger for a year or two still expected that her nephew would return and claim his bride; but he has never done so, nor has there been any correspondence between them. Patience Woolsworthy had learned her lesson dearly. She had given her whole heart to the man; and, though she so bore herself that no one was aware of the violence of the struggle, nevertheless the struggle within her bosom was very violent. She never told herself that she had done wrong; she never regretted her loss; but yet – yet! – the loss was very hard to bear. He also had loved her, but he was not capable of a love which could much injure his daily peace. Her daily peace was gone for many a day to come.

Her father is still living; but there is a curate now in the parish. In conjunction with him and with Miss Le Smyrger she spends her time in the concerns of the parish. In her own eyes she is a confirmed old maid; and such is my opinion also. The romance of her life was played out in that summer. She never sits now lonely on the hill-side thinking how much she might do for one whom she really loved. But with a large heart she loves many, and, with no romance, she works hard to lighten the burdens of those she loves.

As for Captain Broughton, all the world knows that he did marry that great heiress with whom his name was once before connected, and that he is now a useful member of Parliament, working on committees three or four days a week with a zeal that is indefatigable. Sometimes, not often, as he thinks of Patience Woolsworthy, a gratified smile comes across his face.

THE COURTSHIP OF SUSAN BELL

John Munroe Bell had been a lawyer in Albany, State of New York, and as such had thriven well. He had thriven well as long as thrift and thriving on this earth had been allowed to him. But the Almighty had seen fit to shorten his span.

Early in life he had married a timid, anxious, pretty, good little wife, whose whole heart and mind had been given up to do his bidding and deserve his love. She had not only deserved it but had possessed it, and as long as John Munroe Bell had lived, Henrietta Bell – Hetta as he called her – had been a woman rich in blessings. After twelve years of such blessings he had left her, and had left with her two daughters, a second Hetta, and the heroine of our little story, Susan Bell.

A lawyer in Albany may thrive passing well for eight or ten years, and yet not leave behind him any very large sum of money if he dies at the end of that time. Some small modicum, some few thousand dollars, John Bell had amassed, so that his widow and daughters were not absolutely driven to look for work or bread.

In those happy days when cash had begun to flow in plenteously to the young father of the family, he had taken it into his head to build for himself, or rather for his young female brood, a small neat house in the outskirts of Saratoga Springs. In doing so he was instigated as much by the excellence of the investment for his pocket as by the salubrity of the place for his girls. He furnished the house well, and then during some summer weeks his wife lived there, and sometimes he let it.

How the widow grieved when the lord of her heart and master of her mind was laid in the grave, I need not tell. She had already counted ten years of widowhood, and her children had grown to be young women beside her at the time of which I am now about to speak. Since that sad day on which they had left Albany they had lived together at the cottage at the Springs. In winter their life had been lonely enough; but as soon as the hot weather began to drive the fainting citizens out from New York, they had always received two or three boarders – old ladies generally, and occasionally an old gentleman – persons of very steady habits, with whose pockets the widow's moderate demands agreed better than the hotel charges. And so the Bells lived for ten years.

That Saratoga is a gay place in July, August, and September the world knows well enough. To girls who go there with trunks full of muslin and crinoline, for whom a carriage and pair of horses is always waiting immediately after dinner, whose fathers' pockets are bursting with dollars, it is a very gay place. Dancing and flirtations come as a matter of course, and matrimony follows after with only too great rapidity. But the place was not very gay for Hetta or Susan Bell.

In the first place the widow was a timid woman, and among other fears feared greatly that she should be thought guilty of setting traps for husbands. Poor mothers! how often are they charged with this sin when their honest desires go no further than that their bairns may be 'respectit like the lave.' And then she feared flirtations; flirtations that should be that and nothing more, flirtations that are so destructive of the heart's sweetest essence. She feared love also, though she longed for that as well as feared it; – for her girls, I mean; all such feelings for herself were long laid under ground; – and then, like a timid creature as she was, she had other indefinite fears, and among them a great fear that those girls of hers would be left husbandless, – a phase of life which after her twelve years of bliss she regarded as anything but desirable. But the upshot was, – the upshot of so many fears and such small means, – that Hetta and Susan Bell had but a dull life of it.

Were it not that I am somewhat closely restricted in the number of my pages, I would describe at full the merits and beauties of Hetta and Susan Bell. As it is I can but say a few words. At our period of their lives Hetta was nearly one-and-twenty, and Susan was just nineteen. Hetta was a short, plump, demure young woman, with the softest smoothed hair, and the brownest brightest eyes. She was very useful in the house, good at corn cakes, and thought much, particularly in these latter months, of her religious duties. Her sister in the privacy of their own little room would sometimes twit her with the admiring patience with which she would listen to the lengthened eloquence of Mr. Phineas Beckard, the Baptist minister. Now Mr. Phineas Beckard was a bachelor.

Susan was not so good a girl in the kitchen or about the house as was her sister; but she was bright in the parlour, and if that motherly heart could have been made to give out its inmost secret – which, however, it could not have been made to give out in any way painful to dear Hetta – perhaps it might have been found that Susan was loved with the closest love. She was taller than her sister, and lighter; her eyes were blue as were her mother's; her hair was brighter than Hetta's but not always so singularly neat. She had a dimple on her chin, whereas Hetta had none; dimples on her cheeks too, when she smiled; and, oh, such a mouth! There; my allowance of pages permits no more.

One piercing cold winter's day there came knocking at the widow's door – a young man. Winter days, when the ice of January is refrozen by the wind of February, are very cold at Saratoga Springs. In these days there was not often much to disturb the serenity of Mrs. Bell's house; but on the day in question there came knocking at the door – a young man.

Mrs. Bell kept an old domestic, who had lived with them in those happy Albany days. Her name was Kate O'Brien, but though picturesque in name she was hardly so in person. She was a thick-set, noisy, good-natured old Irishwoman, who had joined her lot to that of Mrs. Bell when the latter first began housekeeping, and knowing when she was well off, had remained in the same place from that day forth. She had known Hetta as a baby, and, so to say, had seen Susan's birth.

'And what might you be wanting, sir?' said Kate O'Brien, apparently not quite pleased as she opened the door and let in all the cold air.

'I wish to see Mrs. Bell. Is not this Mrs. Bell's house?' said the young man, shaking the snow from out of the breast of his coat.

He did see Mrs. Bell, and we will now tell who he was, and why he had come, and how it came to pass that his carpet-bag was brought down to the widow's house and one of the front bedrooms was prepared for him, and that he drank tea that night in the widow's parlour.

His name was Aaron Dunn, and by profession he was an engineer. What peculiar misfortune in those days of frost and snow had befallen the line of rails which runs from Schenectady to Lake Champlain, I never quite understood. Banks and bridges had in some way come to grief, and on Aaron Dunn's shoulders was thrown the burden of seeing that they were duly repaired. Saratoga Springs was the centre of these mishaps, and therefore at Saratoga Springs it was necessary that he should take up his temporary abode.

Now there was at that time in New York city a Mr. Bell, great in railway matters – an uncle of the once thriving but now departed Albany lawyer. He was a rich man, but he liked his riches himself; or at any rate had not found himself called upon to share them with the widow and daughters of his nephew. But when it chanced to come to pass that he had a hand in despatching Aaron Dunn to Saratoga, he took the young man aside and recommended him to lodge with the widow. 'There,' said he, 'show her my card.' So much the rich uncle thought he might vouchsafe to do for the nephew's widow.

Mrs. Bell and both her daughters were in the parlour when Aaron Dunn was shown in, snow and all. He told his story in a rough, shaky voice, for his teeth chattered; and he gave the card, almost wishing that he had gone to the empty big hotel, for the widow's welcome was not at first quite warm.

The widow listened to him as he gave his message, and then she took the card and looked at it. Hetta, who was sitting on the side of the fireplace facing the door, went on demurely with her work. Susan gave one glance round – her back was to the stranger – and then another; and then she moved her chair a little nearer to the wall, so as to give the young man room to come to the fire, if he would. He did not come, but his eyes glanced upon Susan Bell; and he thought that the old man in New York was right, and that the big hotel would be cold and dull. It was a pretty face to look on that cold evening as she turned it up from the stocking she was mending.

'Perhaps you don't wish to take winter boarders, ma'am?' said Aaron Dunn.

'We never have done so yet, sir,' said Mrs. Bell timidly. 'Could she let this young wolf in among her lamb-fold? He might be a wolf; – who could tell?'

'Mr. Bell seemed to think it would suit,' said Aaron.

Had he acquiesced in her timidity and not pressed the point, it would have been all up with him. But the widow did not like to go against the big uncle; and so she said, 'Perhaps it may, sir.'

'I guess it will, finely,' said Aaron. And then the widow seeing that the matter was so far settled, put down her work and came round into the passage. Hetta followed her, for there would be house-work to do. Aaron gave himself another shake, settled the weekly number of dollars – with very little difficulty on his part, for he had caught another glance at Susan's face; and then went after his bag. 'Twas thus that Aaron Dunn obtained an entrance into Mrs. Bell's house. 'But what if he be a wolf?' she said to herself over and over again that night, though not exactly in those words. Ay, but there is another side to that question. What if he be a stalwart man, honest-minded, with clever eye, cunning hand, ready brain, broad back, and warm heart; in want of a wife mayhap; a man that can earn his own bread and another's – half a dozen others, when the half-dozen come? Would not that be a good sort of lodger? Such a question as that too did flit, just flit, across the widow's sleepless mind. But then she thought so much more of the wolf! Wolves, she had taught herself to think, were more common than stalwart, honest-minded, wife-desirous men.

'I wonder mother consented to take him,' said Hetta when they were in the little room together.

'And why shouldn't she?' said Susan. 'It will be a help.'

'Yes, it will be a little help,' said Hetta. 'But we have done very well hitherto without winter lodgers.'

'But uncle Bell said she was to.'

'What is uncle Bell to us?' said Hetta, who had a spirit of her own. And she began to surmise within herself whether Aaron Dunn would join the Baptist congregation, and whether Phineas Beckard would approve of this new move.

'He is a very well-behaved young man, at any rate,' said Susan, 'and he draws beautifully. Did you see those things he was doing?'

'He draws very well, I dare say,' said Hetta, who regarded this as but a poor warranty for good behaviour. Hetta also had

some fear of wolves – not for herself, perhaps; but for her
sister.

Aaron Dunn's work – the commencement of his work –
lay at some distance from the Springs, and he left every
morning with a lot of workmen by an early train – almost
before daylight. And every morning, cold and wintry as the
mornings were, the widow got him his breakfast with her
own hands. She took his dollars and would not leave him
altogether to the awkward mercies of Kate O'Brien; nor
would she trust her girls to attend upon the young man.
Hetta she might have trusted; but then Susan would have
asked why she was spared her share of such hardship.

In the evening, leaving his work when it was dark, Aaron
always returned, and then the evening was passed together.
But they were passed with the most demure propriety. These
women would make the tea, cut the bread and butter, and
then sew; while Aaron Dunn, when the cups were removed,
would always go to his plans and drawings.

On Sundays they were more together; but even on this
day there was cause of separation, for Aaron went to the
Episcopalian church, rather to the disgust of Hetta. In the
afternoon however they were together; and then Phineas
Beckard came in to tea on Sundays, and he and Aaron got to
talking on religion; and though they disagreed pretty much
and would not give an inch either one or the other, nevertheless the minister told the widow, and Hetta too probably,
that the lad had good stuff in him, though he was so stiff-
necked.

'But he should be more modest in talking on such matters
with a minister,' said Hetta.

The Rev. Phineas acknowledged that perhaps he should;
but he was honest enough to repeat that the lad had stuff in
him. 'Perhaps after all he is not a wolf,' said the widow to
herself.

Things went on in this way for above a month. Aaron had
declared to himself over and over again that that face was
sweet to look upon, and had unconsciously promised to
himself certain delights in talking and perhaps walking with
the owner of it. But the walkings had not been achieved –
not even the talkings as yet. The truth was that Dunn was

bashful with young women, though he could be so stiff-necked with the minister.

And then he felt angry with himself, inasmuch as he had advanced no further; and as he lay in his bed – which perhaps those pretty hands had helped to make – he resolved that he would be a thought bolder in his bearing. He had no idea of making love to Susan Bell; of course not. But why should he not amuse himself by talking to a pretty girl when she sat so near him, evening after evening?

'What a very quiet young man he is,' said Susan to her sister.

'He has his bread to earn, and sticks to his work,' said Hetta. 'No doubt he has his amusement when he is in the city,' added the elder sister, not wishing to leave too strong an impression of the young man's virtue.

They had all now their settled places in the parlour. Hetta sat on one side of the fire, close to the table, having that side to herself. There she sat always busy. She must have made every dress and bit of linen worn in the house, and hemmed every sheet and towel, so busy was she always. Sometimes, once in a week or so, Phineas Beckard would come in, and then place was made for him between Hetta's usual seat and the table. For when there he would read out loud. On the other side, close also to the table, sat the widow, busy, but not savagely busy as her elder daughter. Between Mrs. Bell and the wall, with her feet ever on the fender, Susan used to sit; not absolutely idle, but doing work of some slender pretty sort, and talking ever and anon to her mother. Opposite to them all, at the other side of the table, far away from the fire, would Aaron Dunn place himself with his plans and drawings before him.

'Are you a judge of bridges, ma'am?' said Aaron, the evening after he had made his resolution. 'Twas thus he began his courtship.

'Of bridges!' said Mrs. Bell – 'oh dear, no, sir.' But she put out her hand to take the little drawing which Aaron handed to her.

'Because that's one I've planned for our bit of a new branch from Moreau up to Lake George. I guess Miss Susan knows something about bridges.'

'I guess I don't,' said Susan – 'only that they oughtn't to tumble down when the frost comes.'

'Ha, ha, ha; no more they ought. I'll tell McEvoy that.' McEvoy had been a former engineer on the line. 'Well, that won't burst with any frost, I guess.'

'Oh, my! how pretty!' said the widow, and then Susan of course jumped up to look over her mother's shoulder.

The artful dodger! He had drawn and coloured a beautiful little sketch of a bridge; not an engineer's plan with sections and measurements, vexatious to a woman's eye, but a graceful little bridge and a string of cars running under it. You could almost hear the bell going.

'Well that is a pretty bridge,' said Susan. 'Isn't it, Hetta?'

'I don't know anything about bridges,' said Hetta, to whose clever eyes the dodge was quite apparent. But in spite of her cleverness Mrs. Bell and Susan had soon moved their chairs round to the table, and were looking through the contents of Aaron's portfolio. 'But yet he may be a wolf,' thought the poor widow, just as she was kneeling down to say her prayers.

That evening certainly made a commencement. Though Hetta went on pertinaciously with the body of a new dress, the other two ladies did not put in another stitch that night. From his drawings Aaron got to his instruments, and before bedtime was teaching Susan how to draw parallel lines. Susan found that she had quite an aptitude for parallel lines, and altogether had a good time of it that evening. It is dull to go on week after week, and month after month talking only to one's mother and sister. It is dull though one does not oneself recognize it to be so. A little change in such matters is so very pleasant. Susan had not the slightest idea of regarding Aaron as even a possible lover. But young ladies do like the conversation of young gentlemen. Oh, my exceedingly proper, prim, old lady, you who are so shocked at this as a general doctrine, has it never occurred to you that the Creator has so intended it?

Susan, understanding little of the how and why, knew that she had had a good time, and was rather in spirits as she went to bed. But Hetta had been frightened by the dodge.

'Oh, Hetta you should have looked at those drawings. He is so clever!' said Susan.

'I don't know that they would have done me much good,'
replied Hetta.

'Good! Well, they'd do me more good than a long sermon,
I know,' said Susan; 'except on a Sunday, of course,' she
added apologetically. This was an ill-tempered attack both on
Hetta and Hetta's admirer. But then why had Hetta been so
snappish?

'I'm sure he's a wolf,' thought Hetta as she went to bed.

'What a very clever young man he is!' thought Susan to
herself as she pulled the warm clothes round about her
shoulders and ears.

'Well; that certainly was an improvement,' thought Aaron
as he went through the same operation, with a stronger
feeling of self-approbation than he had enjoyed for some time
past.

In the course of the next fortnight the family arrangements
all altered themselves. Unless when Beckard was there Aaron
would sit in the widow's place, the widow would take Susan's
chair, and the two girls would be opposite. And then Dunn
would read to them; not sermons, but passages from
Shakespeare, and Byron, and Longfellow. 'He reads much
better than Mr. Beckard,' Susan had said one night. 'Of
course you're a competent judge!' had been Hetta's retort. 'I
mean that I like it better,' said Susan. 'It's well that all people
don't think alike,' replied Hetta.

And then there was a deal of talking. The widow herself, as
unconscious in this respect as her youngest daughter, certainly
did find that a little variety was agreeable on those long winter
nights; and talked herself with unaccustomed freedom. And
Beckard came there oftener and talked very much. When he
was there the two young men did all the talking, and they
pounded each other immensely. But still there grew up a sort
of friendship between them.

'Mr. Beckard seems quite to take to him,' said Mrs. Bell to
her eldest daughter.

'It is his great good nature, mother,' replied Hetta.

It was at the end of the second month when Aaron took
another step in advance – a perilous step. Sometimes on
evenings he still went on with his drawing for an hour or so;
but during three or four evenings he never asked any one to

look at what he was doing. On one Friday he sat over his work till late, without any reading or talking at all; so late that at last Mrs. Bell said 'If you're going to sit much longer, Mr. Dunn, I'll get you to put out the candles.' Thereby showing, had he known it or had she, that the mother's confidence in the young man was growing fast. Hetta knew all about it, and dreaded that the growth was too quick.

'I've finished now,' said Aaron; and he looked carefully at the card-board on which he had been washing in his water-colours. 'I've finished now.' He then hesitated a moment; but ultimately he put the card into his portfolio and carried it up to his bedroom. Who does not perceive that it was intended as a present to Susan Bell?

The question which Aaron asked himself that night, and which he hardly knew how to answer was this. Should he offer the drawing to Susan in the presence of her mother and sister, or on some occasion when they two might be alone together? No such occasion had ever yet occurred, but Aaron thought that it might probably be brought about. But then he wanted to make no fuss about it. His first intention had been to chuck the drawing lightly across the table when it was completed, and so make nothing of it. But he had finished it with more care than he had at first intended; and then he had hesitated when he had finished it. It was too late now for that plan of chucking it over the table.

On the Saturday evening when he came down from his room, Mr. Beckard was there, and there was no opportunity that night. On the Sunday, in conformity with a previous engagement, he went to hear Mr. Beckard preach, and walked to and from meeting with the family. This pleased Mrs. Bell, and they were all very gracious that afternoon. But Sunday was no day for the picture.

On Monday the thing had become of importance to him. Things always do when they are kept over. Before tea that evening when he came down Mrs. Bell and Susan only were in the room. He knew Hetta for his foe, and therefore determined to use this occasion.

'Miss Susan,' he said, stammering somewhat, and blushing too, poor fool! 'I have done a little drawing which I want you to accept,' and he put his portfolio down on the table.

'Oh! I don't know,' said Susan who had seen the blush.

Mrs. Bell had seen the blush also, and pursed her mouth up, and looked grave. Had there been no stammering and no blush, she might have thought nothing of it.

Aaron saw at once that his little gift was not to go down smoothly. He was however in for it now, so he picked it out from among the other papers in the case and brought it over to Susan. He endeavoured to hand it to her with an air of indifference, but I cannot say that he succeeded.

It was a very pretty well-finished, water-coloured drawing, representing still the same bridge, but with more adjuncts. In Susan's eyes it was a work of high art. Of pictures probably she had seen but little, and her liking for the artist no doubt added to her admiration. But the more she admired it and wished for it, the stronger was her feeling that she ought not to take it.

Poor Susan! she stood for a minute looking at the drawing, but she said nothing; not even a word of praise. She felt that she was red in the face, and uncourteous to their lodger; but her mother was looking at her and she did not know how to behave herself.

Mrs. Bell put out her hand for the sketch, trying to bethink herself as she did so in what least uncivil way she could refuse the present. She took a moment to look at it collecting her thoughts, and as she did so her woman's wit came to her aid.

'Oh dear, Mr. Dunn, it is very pretty; quite a beautiful picture. I cannot let Susan rob you of that. You must keep that for some of your own particular friends.'

'But I did it for her,' said Aaron innocently.

Susan looked down at the ground, half pleased at the declaration. The drawing would look very pretty in a small gilt frame put over her dressing-table. But the matter now was altogether in her mother's hands.

'I am afraid it is too valuable, sir, for Susan to accept.'

'It is not valuable at all,' said Aaron, declining to take it back from the widow's hand.

'Oh, I am quite sure it is. It is worth ten dollars at least – or twenty,' said poor Mrs. Bell, not in the very best taste. But she was perplexed and did not know how to get out of the scrape. The article in question now lay upon the table-cloth, appropriated by no one, and at this moment Hetta came into the room.

'It is not worth ten cents,' said Aaron, with something like a frown on his brow. 'But as we had been talking about the bridge, I thought Miss Susan would accept it.'

'Accept what?' said Hetta. And then her eye fell upon the drawing and she took it up.

'It is beautifully done,' said Mrs. Bell, wishing much to soften the matter; perhaps the more so, that Hetta the demure was now present. 'I am telling Mr. Dunn that we can't take a present of anything so valuable.'

'Oh dear, no,' said Hetta. 'It wouldn't be right.'

It was a cold frosty evening in March, and the fire was burning brightly on the hearth. Aaron Dunn took up the drawing quietly – very quietly – and rolling it up, as such drawings are rolled, put it between the blazing logs. It was the work of four evenings, and his chef-d'œuvre in the way of art.

Susan, when she saw what he had done, burst out into tears. The widow could very readily have done so also, but she was able to refrain herself, and merely exclaimed – 'Oh, Mr. Dunn!'

'If Mr. Dunn chooses to burn his own picture, he has certainly a right to do so,' said Hetta.

Aaron immediately felt ashamed of what he had done; and he also could have cried, but for his manliness. He walked away to one of the parlour-windows, and looked out upon the frosty night. It was dark, but the stars were bright, and he thought that he should like to be walking fast by himself along the line of rails towards Balston. There he stood, perhaps for three minutes. He thought it would be proper to give Susan time to recover from her tears.

'Will you please to come to your tea, sir?' said the soft voice of Mrs. Bell.

He turned round to do so, and found that Susan was gone. It was not quite in her power to recover from her tears in three minutes. And then the drawing had been so beautiful! It had been done expressly for her too! And there had been something, she knew not what, in his eye as he had so declared. She had watched him intently over those four evenings' work, wondering why he did not show it, till her feminine curiosity had become rather strong. It was something very particular, she was sure, and she had learned that all that precious work had been for her. Now all that precious work was destroyed. How was it possible that she should not cry for more than three minutes?

The others took their meal in perfect silence, and when it was over the two women sat down to their work. Aaron had a book which he pretended to read, but instead of reading he was bethinking himself that he had behaved badly. What right had he to throw them all into such confusion by indulging in his passion? He was ashamed of what he had done, and fancied that Susan would hate him. Fancying that, he began to find at the same time that he by no means hated her.

At last Hetta got up and left the room. She knew that her sister was sitting alone in the cold, and Hetta was affectionate. Susan had not been in fault, and therefore Hetta went up to console her.

'Mrs. Bell,' said Aaron, as soon as the door was closed, 'I beg your pardon for what I did just now.'

'Oh, sir, I'm so sorry that the picture is burnt,' said poor Mrs. Bell.

'The picture does not matter a straw,' said Aaron. 'But I see that I have disturbed you all, – and I am afraid I have made Miss Susan unhappy.'

'She was grieved because your picture was burnt,' said Mrs. Bell, putting some emphasis on the 'your,' intending to show that her daughter had not regarded the drawing as her own. But the emphasis bore another meaning; and so the widow perceived as soon as she had spoken.

'Oh, I can do twenty more of the same if anybody wanted them,' said Aaron. 'If I do another like it, will you let her take it, Mrs. Bell? – just to show that you have forgiven me, and that we are friends as we were before?'

Was he, or was he not a wolf? That was the question which Mrs. Bell scarcely knew how to answer. Hetta had given her voice, saying he was lupine. Mr. Beckard's opinion she had not liked to ask directly. Mr. Beckard she thought would probably propose to Hetta; but as yet he had not done so. And, as he was still a stranger in the family, she did not like in any way to compromise Susan's name. Indirectly she had asked the question, and, indirectly also, Mr. Beckard's answer had been favourable.

'But it mustn't mean anything, sir,' was the widow's weak answer, when she had paused on the question for a moment.

'Oh no, of course not,' said Aaron, joyously, and his face became radiant and happy. 'And I do beg your pardon for burning it; and the young ladies' pardon too.' And then he rapidly got out his card-board, and set himself to work about another bridge. The widow meditating many things in her heart, commenced the hemming of a handkerchief.

In about an hour the two girls came back to the room and silently took their accustomed places. Aaron hardly looked up, but went on diligently with his drawing. This bridge should be a better bridge than that other. Its acceptance was now assured. Of course it was to mean nothing. That was a matter of course. So he worked away diligently, and said nothing to anybody.

When they went off to bed the two girls went into the mother's room. 'Oh, mother, I hope he is not very angry,' said Susan.

'Angry!' said Hetta, 'if anybody should be angry, it is mother. He ought to have known that Susan could not accept it. He should never have offered it.'

'But he's doing another,' said Mrs. Bell.

'Not for her,' said Hetta.

'Yes he is,' said Mrs. Bell, 'and I have promised that she shall take it.' Susan as she heard this sank gently into the chair behind her, and her eyes became full of tears. The intimation was almost too much for her.

'Oh mother!' said Hetta.

'But I particularly said that it was to mean nothing.'

'Oh mother, that makes it worse.'

Why should Hetta interfere in this way, thought Susan to herself. Had she interfered when Mr. Beckard gave Hetta a testament bound in morocco? Had not she smiled, and looked gratified, and kissed her sister, and declared that Phineas Beckard was a nice dear man, and by far the most elegant preacher at the Springs? Why should Hetta be so cruel?

'I don't see that, my dear,' said the mother. Hetta would not explain before her sister, so they all went to bed.

On the Thursday evening the drawing was finished. Not a word had been said about it, at any rate in his presence, and he had gone on working in silence. 'There,' said he, late on the Thursday evening, 'I don't know that it will be any better if I go on daubing for another hour. There, Miss Susan; there's another bridge. I hope that will neither burst with the frost, nor yet be destroyed by fire,' and he gave it a light flip with his fingers and sent it skimming over the table.

Susan blushed and smiled, and took it up. 'Oh, it is beautiful,' she said. 'Isn't it beautifully done, mother?' and then all the three got up to look at it, and all confessed that it was excellently done.

'And I am sure we are very much obliged to you,' said Susan after a pause, remembering that she had not yet thanked him.

'Oh, it's nothing,' said he, not quite liking the word 'we.'

On the following day he returned from his work to Saratoga about noon. This he had never done before, and therefore no one expected that he would be seen in the house before the evening. On this occasion however he went straight thither, and as chance would have it, both the widow and her elder daughter were out. Susan was there alone in charge of the house.

He walked in and opened the parlour door. There she sat, with her feet on the fender, with her work unheeded on the table behind her, and the picture, Aaron's drawing, lying on her knees. She was gazing at it intently as he entered, thinking in her young heart that it possessed all the beauties which a picture could possess.

'Oh, Mr. Dunn,' she said getting up and holding the tell-tale sketch behind the skirt of her dress.

'Miss Susan, I have come here to tell your mother that I must start for New York this afternoon and be there for six weeks, or perhaps longer.'

'Mother is out,' said she; 'I'm so sorry.'

'Is she?' said Aaron.

'And Hetta too. Dear me. And you'll be wanting dinner. I'll go and see about it.'

Aaron began to swear that he could not possibly eat any dinner. He had dined once, and was going to dine again; – anything to keep her from going.

'But you must have something, Mr. Dunn,' and she walked towards the door.

But he put his back to it. 'Miss Susan,' said he, 'I guess I've been here nearly two months.'

'Yes sir, I believe you have,' she replied, shaking in her shoes and not knowing which way to look.

'And I hope we have been good friends.'

'Yes, sir,' said Susan, almost beside herself as to what she was saying.

'I'm going away now, and it seems to be such a time before I'll be back.'

'Will it, sir?'

'Six weeks, Miss Susan!' and then he paused, looking into her eyes, to see what he could read there. She leant against the table, pulling to pieces a morsel of half ravelled muslin which she held in her hand; but her eyes were turned to the ground, and he could hardly see them.

'Miss Susan,' he continued, 'I may as well speak out now as at another time.' He too was looking towards the ground, and clearly did not know what to do with his hands. 'The truth is just this. I – I love you dearly, with all my heart. I never saw any one I ever thought so beautiful, so nice, and so good; – and what's more, I never shall. I'm not very good at this sort of thing, I know; but I couldn't go away from Saratoga for six weeks and not tell you. And then he ceased. He did not ask for any love in return. His presumption had not got so far as that yet. He merely declared his passion, leaning against the door, and there he stood twiddling his thumbs.

Susan had not the slightest conception of the way in which she ought to receive such a declaration. She had never had a lover before; nor had she ever thought of Aaron absolutley as a lover, though something very like love for him had been crossing over her spirit. Now, at this moment, she felt that he was the beau-idéal of manhood, though his boots were covered with the railway mud, and though his pantaloons were tucked up in rolls round his ankles. He was a fine, well-grown, open-faced fellow, whose eye was bold and yet tender, whose brow was full and broad, and all his bearing manly. Love him! Of course she loved him. Why else had her heart melted with pleasure when her mother said that that second picture was to be accepted?

But what was she to say? Anything but the open truth; she well knew that. The open truth would not do at all. What would her mother say and Hetta if she were rashly to say that? Hetta, she knew, would be dead against such a lover, and of her mother's approbation she had hardly more hope. Why they should disapprove of Aaron as a lover she had never asked herself. There are many nice things that seem to be wrong only because they are so nice. Maybe that Susan regarded a lover as one of them. 'Oh, Mr. Dunn, you shouldn't.' That in fact was all that she could say.

'Should not I?' said he. 'Well, perhaps not; but there's the truth, and no harm ever comes of that. Perhaps I'd better not ask you for an answer now, but I thought it better you should know it all. And remember this – I only care for one thing now in the world, and that is for your love.' And then he paused, thinking possibly that in spite of what he had said he might perhaps get some sort of an answer, some inkling of the state of her heart's disposition towards him.

But Susan had at once resolved to take him at his word when he suggested that an immediate reply was not necessary. To say that she loved him was of course impossible, and to say that she did not was equally so. She determined therefore to close at once with the offer of silence.

When he ceased speaking there was a moment's pause, during which he strove hard to read what might be written on her down-turned face. But he was not good at such reading. 'Well, I guess I'll go and get my things ready now,' he said, and then turned round to open the door.

'Mother will be in before you are gone, I suppose,' said Susan.

'I have only got twenty minutes,' said he, looking at his watch. 'But, Susan, tell her what I have said to you. Good-bye.' And he put out his hand. He knew he should see her again, but this had been his plan to get her hand in his.

'Good-bye, Mr. Dunn,' and she gave him her hand.

He held it tight for a moment, so that she could not draw it away, – could not if she would. 'Will you tell your mother?' he asked.

'Yes,' she answered, quite in a whisper. 'I guess I'd better tell her.' And then she gave a long sigh. He pressed her hand again and got it up to his lips.

'Mr. Dunn, don't,' she said. But he did kiss it. 'God bless you, my own dearest, dearest girl! I'll just open the door as I come down. Perhaps Mrs. Bell will be here.' And then he rushed up stairs.

But Mrs. Bell did not come in. She and Hetta were at a weekly service at Mr. Beckard's meeting-house, and Mr. Beckard it seemed had much to say. Susan, when left alone, sat down and tried to think. But she could not think; she could only love. She could use her mind only in recounting to herself the perfections of that demigod whose heavy steps were so audible overhead, as he walked to and fro collecting his things and putting them into his bag.

And then, just when he had finished, she bethought herself that he must be hungry. She flew to the kitchen, but she was too late. Before she could even reach at the loaf of bread he descended the stairs with a clattering noise, and heard her voice as she spoke quickly to Kate O'Brien.

'Miss Susan,' he said, 'don't get anything for me, for I'm off.'

'Oh, Mr. Dunn, I am so sorry. You'll be so hungry on your journey,' and she came out to him in the passage.

'I shall want nothing on the journey, dearest, if you'll say one kind word to me.'

Again her eyes went to the ground. 'What do you want me to say, Mr. Dunn?'

'Say, God bless you, Aaron.'

'God bless you, Aaron,' said she; and yet she was sure that she had not declared her love. He however thought otherwise, and went up to New York with a happy heart.

Things happened in the next fortnight rather quickly. Susan at once resolved to tell her mother, but she resolved also not to tell Hetta. That afternoon she got her mother to herself in Mrs. Bell's own room, and then she made a clean breast of it.

'And what did you say to him, Susan?'

'I said nothing, mother.'

'Nothing, dear!'

'No, mother; not a word. He told me he didn't want it.' She forgot how she had used his Christian name in bidding God bless him.

'Oh, dear!' said the widow.

'Was it very wrong?' asked Susan.

'But what do you think yourself, my child?' asked Mrs. Bell after a while. 'What are your own feelings?'

Mrs. Bell was sitting on a chair, and Susan was standing opposite to her against the post of the bed. She made no answer, but moving from her place, she threw herself into her mother's arms, and hid her face on her mother's shoulder. It was easy enough to guess what were her feelings.

'But, my darling,' said her mother, 'you must not think that it is an engagement.'

'No,' said Susan, sorrowfully.

'Young men say those things to amuse themselves.' Wolves, she would have said, had she spoken out her mind freely.

'Oh, mother, he is not like that.'

The daughter contrived to extract a promise from the mother that Hetta should not be told just at present. Mrs. Bell calculated that she had six weeks before her; as yet Mr. Beckard had not spoken out, but there was reason to suppose that he would do so before those six weeks would be over, and then she would be able to seek counsel from him.

Mr. Beckard spoke out at the end of six days, and Hetta frankly accepted him. 'I hope you'll love your brother-in-law,' said she to Susan.

'Oh, I will indeed,' said Susan; and in the softness of her heart at the moment she almost made up her mind to tell; but Hetta was full of her own affairs, and thus it passed off.

It was then arranged that Hetta should go and spend a week with Mr. Beckard's parents. Old Mr. Beckard was a farmer living near Utica, and now that the match was declared and approved, it was thought well that Hetta should know her future husband's family. So she went for a week, and Mr. Beckard went with her. 'He will be back in plenty of time for me to speak to him before Aaron Dunn's six weeks are over,' said Mrs. Bell to herself.

But things did not go exactly as she expected. On the very morning after the departure of the engaged couple, there came a letter from Aaron, saying that he would be at Saratoga that very evening. The railway people had ordered him down again for some days' special work; then he was to go elsewhere and not to return to Saratoga till June. 'But he hoped,' so said the letter, 'that Mrs. Bell would not turn him into the street even then, though the summer might have come, and her regular lodgers might be expected.'

'Oh dear, oh dear!' said Mrs. Bell to herself, reflecting that she had no one of whom she could ask advice, and that she must decide that very day. Why had she let Mr. Beckard go without telling him? Then she told Susan, and Susan spent the day trembling. Perhaps, thought Mrs. Bell, he will say nothing about it. In such case, however, would it not be her duty to say something? Poor mother! She trembled nearly as much as Susan.

It was dark when the fatal knock came at the door. The tea-things were already laid, and the tea-cake was already baked; for it would at any rate be necessary to give Mr. Dunn his tea. Susan, when she heard the knock, rushed from her chair and took refuge up stairs. The widow gave a long sigh, and settled her dress. Kate O'Brien with willing step opened the door, and bade her old friend welcome.

'How are the ladies?' asked Aaron, trying to gather something from the face and voice of the domestic.

'Miss Hetta and Mr. Beckard be gone off to Utica, just man-and-wife like; and so they are, more power to them.'

'Oh indeed: I'm very glad,' said Aaron – and so he was; very glad to have Hetta the demure out of the way. And then he made his way into the parlour, doubting much, and hoping much.

Mrs. Bell rose from her chair, and tried to look grave. Aaron glancing round the room saw that Susan was not there. He walked straight up to the widow, and offered her his hand, which she took. It might be that Susan had not thought fit to tell, and in such case it would not be right for him to compromise her; so he said never a word.

But the subject was too important to the mother to allow her being silent when the young man stood before her. 'Oh, Mr. Dunn,' said she, 'what is this you have been saying to Susan?'

'I have asked her to be my wife,' said he, drawing himself up and looking her full in the face. Mrs. Bell's heart was almost as soft as her daughter's, and it was nearly gone; but at the moment she had nothing to say but, 'oh dear, oh dear!'

'May I not call you mother?' said he, taking both her hands in his.

'Oh dear – oh dear! But will you be good to her? Oh Aaron Dunn, if you deceive my child!'

In another quarter of an hour, Susan was kneeling at her mother's knee, with her face on her mother's lap; the mother was wiping tears out of her eyes; and Aaron was standing by holding one of the widow's hands.

'You are my mother too, now,' said he. What would Hetta and Mr. Beckard say, when they came back? But then he surely was not a wolf!

There were four or five days left for courtship before Hetta and Mr. Beckard would return; four or five days during which Susan might be happy, Aaron triumphant, and Mrs. Bell nervous. Days I have said, but after all it was only the evenings that were so left. Every morning Susan got up to give Aaron his breakfast, but Mrs. Bell got up also. Susan boldly declared her right to do so, and Mrs. Bell found no objection which she could urge. But after that Aaron was always absent till seven or eight in the evening, when he would return to his tea. Then came the hour or two of lovers' intercourse.

But they were very tame, those hours. The widow still felt an undefined fear that she was wrong, and though her heart yearned to know that her daughter was happy in the sweet happiness of accepted love, yet she dreaded to be too confident. Not a word had been said about money matters; not a word of Aaron Dunn's relatives. So she did not leave them by themselves, but waited with what patience she could for the return of her wise counsellors.

And then Susan hardly knew how to behave herself with her accepted suitor. She felt that she was very happy; but perhaps she was most happy when she was thinking about him through the long day, assisting in fixing little things for his comfort, and waiting for his evening return. And as he sat there in the parlour, she could be happy then too, if she were but allowed to sit still and look at him, – not stare at him but raise her eyes every now and again to his face for the shortest possible glance, as she had been used to do ever since he came there.

But he, unconsciable lover, wanted to hear her speak, was desirous of being talked to, and perhaps thought that he should by rights be allowed to sit by her, and hold her hand. No such privileges were accorded to him. If they had been alone together, walking side by side on the green turf, as lovers should walk, she would soon have found the use of her tongue, – have talked fast enough no doubt. Under such circumstances, when a girl's shyness has given way to real intimacy, there is in general no end to her power of chatting. But though there was much love between Aaron and Susan, there was as yet but little intimacy. And then, let a mother be ever so motherly – and no mother could have more of a mother's tenderness than Mrs. Bell – still her presence must be a restraint. Aaron was very fond of Mrs. Bell; but nevertheless he did sometimes wish that some domestic duty would take her out of the parlour for a few happy minutes. Susan went out very often, but Mrs. Bell seemed to be a fixture.

Once for a moment he did find his love alone, immediately as he came into the house. 'My own Susan, you do love me? do say so to me once.' And he contrived to slip his arm round her waist. 'Yes,' she whispered; but she slipped, like an eel, from his hands, and left him only preparing himself for a kiss. And then when she got to her room, half frightened, she clasped her hands together, and bethought herself that she did really love him with a strength and depth of love which filled her whole existence. Why could she not have told him something of all this?

And so the few days of his second sojourn at Saratoga passed away, not altogether satisfactorily. It was settled that he should return to New York on Saturday night, leaving Saratoga on that evening; and as the Beckards – Hetta was already regarded quite as a Beckard – were to be back to dinner on that day, Mrs. Bell would have an opportunity of telling her wondrous tale. It might be well that Mr. Beckard should see Aaron before his departure.

On that Saturday the Beckards did arrive just in time for dinner. It may be imagined that Susan's appetite was not very keen, nor her manner very collected. But all this passed by unobserved in the importance attached to the various Beckard arrangements which came under discussion. Ladies and gentlemen circumstanced as were Hetta and Mr. Beckard are perhaps a little too apt to think that their own affairs are paramount. But after dinner Susan vanished at once, and when Hetta prepared to follow her, desirous of further talk about matrimonial arrangements, her mother stopped her, and the disclosure was made.

'Proposed to her!' said Hetta, who perhaps thought that one marriage in a family was enough at a time.

'Yes, my love – and he did it, I must say, in a very honourable way, telling her not to make any answer till she had spoken to me; – now that was very nice; was it not, Phineas?' Mrs. Bell had become very anxious that Aaron should not be voted a wolf.

'And what has been said to him since?' asked the discreet Phineas.

'Why – nothing absolutely decisive.' Oh, Mrs. Bell! 'You see I know nothing as to his means.'

'Nothing at all,' said Hetta.

'He is a man that will always earn his bread,' said Mr. Beckard; and Mrs. Bell blessed him in her heart for saying it.

'But has he been encouraged?' asked Hetta.

'Well; yes, he has,' said the widow.

'Then Susan I suppose likes him?' asked Phineas.

'Well; yes, she does,' said the widow. And the conference ended in a resolution that Phineas Beckard should have a conversation with Aaron Dunn, as to his worldly means and position; and that he, Phineas, should decide whether Aaron might, or might not be at once accepted as a lover, according to the tenor of that conversation. Poor Susan was not told anything of all this. 'Better not,' said Hetta the demure. 'It will only flurry her the more.' How would she have liked it, if without consulting her, they had left it to Aaron to decide whether or no she might marry Phineas?

They knew where on the works Aaron was to be found, and thither Mr. Beckard rode after dinner. We need not narrate at length the conference between the young men. Aaron at once declared that he had nothing but what he made as an engineer, and explained that he held no permanent situation on the line. He was well paid at that present moment, but at the end of summer he would have to look for employment.

'Then you can hardly marry quite at present,' said the discreet minister.

'Perhaps not quite immediately.'

'And long engagements are never wise,' said the other.

'Three or four months,' suggested Aaron. But Mr. Beckard shook his head.

The afternoon at Mrs. Bell's house was melancholy. The final decision of the three judges was as follows. There was to be no engagement; of course no correspondence. Aaron was to be told that it would be better that he should get lodgings elsewhere when he returned; but that he would be allowed to visit at Mrs. Bell's house, – and at Mrs. Beckard's, which was very considerate. If he should succeed in getting a permanent appointment, and if he and Susan still held the same mind, why then – &c. &c. Such was Susan's fate, as communicated to her by Mrs. Bell and Hetta. She sat still and wept when she heard it; but she did not complain. She had always felt that Hetta would be against her.

'Mayn't I see him, then?' she said through her tears.

Hetta thought she had better not. Mrs. Bell thought she might. Phineas decided that they might shake hands, but only in full conclave. There was to be no lovers' farewell. Aaron was to leave the house at half-past five; but before he went Susan should be called down. Poor Susan! She sat down and bemoaned herself; uncomplaining, but very sad.

Susan was soft, feminine, and manageable. But Aaron Dunn was not very soft, was especially masculine, and in some matters not easily manageable. When Mr. Beckard in the widow's presence – Hetta had retired in obedience to her lover – informed him of the court's decision, there came over his face the look which he had worn when he burned the picture. 'Mrs. Bell,' he said, 'had encouraged his engagement; and he did not understand why other people should now come and disturb it.'

'Not an engagement, Aaron,' said Mrs. Bell piteously.

'He was able and willing to work,' he said, 'and knew his profession. What young man of his age had done better than he had?' and he glanced round at them with perhaps more pride than was quite becoming.

Then Mr. Beckard spoke out, very wisely no doubt, but perhaps a little too much at length. Sons and daughters as well as fathers and mothers will know very well what he said; so I need not repeat his words. I cannot say that Aaron listened with much attention, but he understood perfectly what the upshot of it was. Many a man understands the purport of many a sermon without listening to one word in ten. Mr. Beckard meant to be kind in his manner; indeed was so only that Aaron could not accept as kindness any interference on his part.

'I'll tell you what, Mrs. Bell,' said he. 'I look upon myself as engaged to her. And I look on her as engaged to me. I tell you so fairly; and I believe that's her mind as well as mine.'

'But, Aaron, you won't try to see her – or to write to her, – not in secret; will you?'

'When I try to see her, I'll come and knock at this door; and if I write to her, I'll write to her full address by the post. I never did and never will do anything in secret.'

'I know you're good and honest,' said the widow with her handkerchief to her eyes.

'Then why do you separate us?' asked he, almost roughly. 'I suppose I may see her at any rate before I go. My time's nearly up now, I guess.'

And then Susan was called for, and she and Hetta came down together. Susan crept in behind her sister. Her eyes were red with weeping, and her appearance was altogether disconsolate. She had had a lover for a week, and now she was to be robbed of him.

'Good-bye, Susan,' said Aaron, and he walked up to her without bashfulness or embarrassment. Had they all been compliant and gracious to him he would have been as bashful as his love; but now his temper was hot. 'Good-bye, Susan,' and she took his hand, and he held hers till he had finished. 'And remember this, I look upon you as my promised wife, and I don't fear that you'll deceive me. At any rate I sha'n't deceive you.'

'Good-bye, Aaron,' she sobbed.

'Good-bye, and God bless you, my own darling!' And then without saying a word to any one else, he turned his back upon them and went his way.

There had been something very consolatory, very sweet, to the poor girl in her lover's last words. And yet they had almost made her tremble. He had been so bold, and stern, and confident. He had seemed so utterly to defy the impregnable discretion of Mr. Beckard, so to despise the demure propriety of Hetta. But of this she felt sure, when she came to question her heart, that she could never, never, never cease to love him better than all the world beside. She would wait – patiently if she could find patience – and then, if he deserted her, she would die.

In another month Hetta became Mrs. Beckard. Susan brisked up a little for the occasion, and looked very pretty as bridesmaid. She was serviceable too in arranging household matters, hemming linen and sewing table-cloths; though of course in these matters she did not do a tenth of what Hetta did.

Then the summer came, the Saratoga summer of July, August, and September, during which the widow's house was full; and Susan's hands saved the pain of her heart, for she was forced into occupation. Now that Hetta was gone to her own duties, it was necessary that Susan's part in the household should be more prominent.

Aaron did not come back to his work at Saratoga. Why he did not, they could not then learn. During the whole long summer they heard not a word of him nor from him; and then when the cold winter months came and their boarders had left them, Mrs. Beckard congratulated her sister in that she had given no further encouragement to a lover who cared so little for her. This was very hard to bear. But Susan did bear it.

That winter was very sad. They learned nothing of Aaron Dunn till about January; and then they heard that he was doing very well. He was engaged on the Erie trunk line, was paid highly, and was much esteemed. And yet he neither came nor sent! 'He has an excellent situation,' their informant told them. 'And a permanent one?' asked the widow. 'Oh, yes, no doubt,' said the gentleman, 'for I happen to know that they count greatly on him.' And yet he sent no word of love.

After that the winter became very sad indeed. Mrs. Bell thought it to be her duty now to teach her daughter that in all probability she would see Aaron Dunn no more. It was open to him to leave her without being absolutely a wolf. He had been driven from the house when he was poor, and they had no right to expect that he would return, now that he had made some rise in the world. 'Men do amuse themselves in that way,' the widow tried to teach her.

'He is not like that, mother,' she said again.

'But they do not think so much of these things as we do,' urged the mother.

'Don't they?' said Susan, oh, so sorrowfully; and so through the whole long winter months she became paler and paler, and thinner and thinner.

And then Hetta tried to console her with religion, and that perhaps did not make things any better. Religious consolation is the best cure for all griefs; but it must not be looked for specially with regard to any individual sorrow. A religious man, should he become bankrupt through the misfortunes of the world, will find true consolation in his religion even for that sorrow. But a bankrupt, who has not thought much of such things, will hardly find solace by taking up religion for that special occasion.

And Hetta perhaps was hardly prudent in her attempts. She thought that it was wicked in Susan to grow thin and pale for love of Aaron Dunn, and she hardly hid her thoughts. Susan was not sure but that it might be wicked, but this doubt in no way tended to make her plump or rosy. So that in those days she found no comfort in her sister.

But her mother's pity and soft love did ease her sufferings, though it could not make them cease. Her mother did not tell her that she was wicked, or bid her read long sermons, or force her to go oftener to the meeting-house.

'He will never come again, I think,' she said one day, as with a shawl wrapped around her shoulders, she leant with her head upon her mother's bosom.

'My own darling,' said the mother, pressing her child to her side.

'You think he never will, eh, mother?' What could Mrs. Bell say? In her heart of hearts she did not think he ever would come again.

'No, my child. I do not think he will.' And then the hot tears ran down, and the sobs came thick and frequent.

'My darling, my darling!' exclaimed the mother; and they wept together.

'Was I wicked to love him at the first?' she asked that night.

'No, my child; you were not wicked at all. At least I think not.'

'Then why –' Why was he sent away? It was on her tongue to ask that question; but she paused and spared her mother. This was as they were going to bed. The next morning Susan did not get up. She was not ill, she said; but weak and weary. Would her mother let her lie that day? And then Mrs. Bell went down alone to her room, and sorrowed with all her heart for the sorrow of her child. Why, oh why, had she driven away from her door-sill the love of an honest man?

On the next morning Susan again did not get up; – nor did she hear, or if she heard she did not recognize, the step of the postman who brought a letter to the door. Early, before the widow's breakfast the postman came, and the letter which he brought was as follows:–

'My dear Mrs. Bell,
   'I have now got a permanent situation on the Erie line, and the salary is enough for myself and a wife. At least I think so, and I hope you will too. I shall be down at Saratoga to-morrow evening, and I hope neither Susan nor you will refuse to receive me.
                    'Yours affectionately,
                       'Aaron Dunn.'

That was all. It was very short, and did not contain one word of love; but it made the widow's heart leap for joy. She was rather afraid that Aaron was angry, he wrote so curtly and with such a brusque business-like attention to mere facts; but surely he could have but one object in coming there. And then he alluded specially to a wife. So the widow's heart leapt with joy.

But how was she to tell Susan? She ran up stairs almost breathless with haste, to the bedroom door: but then she stopped: too much joy she had heard was as dangerous as too much sorrow; she must think it over for a while, and so she crept back again.

But after breakfast – that is, when she had sat for a while over her teacup – she returned to the room, and this time she entered it. The letter was in her hand, but held so as to be hidden; – in her left hand as she sat down with her right arm towards the invalid.

'Susan dear,' she said, and smiled at her child, 'you'll be able to get up this morning? eh, dear?'

'Yes, mother,' said Susan, thinking that her mother objected to this idleness of her lying in bed. And so she began to bestir herself.

'I don't mean this very moment, love. Indeed, I want to sit with you for a little while,' and she put her right arm affectionately round her daughter's waist.

'Dearest mother,' said Susan.

'Ah! there's one dearer than me, I guess,' and Mrs. Bell smiled sweetly, as she made the maternal charge against her daughter.

Susan raised herself quickly in the bed, and looked straight into her mother's face. 'Mother, mother,' she said, 'What is it? You've something to tell, Oh, mother!' And stretching herself over, she struck her hand against the corner of Aaron's letter. 'Mother, you've a letter. Is he coming, mother?' and with eager eyes and open lips, she sat up, holding tight to her mother's arm.

'Yes, love. I have got a letter.'

'Is he – is he coming?'

How the mother answered, I can hardly tell; but she did answer, and they were soon lying in each other's arms, warm with each other's tears. It was almost hard to say which was the happier.

Aaron was to be there that evening – that very evening. 'Oh, mother, let me get up,' said Susan.

But Mrs. Bell said no, not yet; her darling was pale and thin, and she almost wished that Aaron was not coming for another week. What if he should come and look at her, and finding her beauty gone, vanish again and seek a wife elsewhere!

So Susan lay in bed, thinking of her happiness, dozing now and again, and fearing as she waked that it was a dream, looking constantly at that drawing of his, which she kept outside upon the bed, nursing her love and thinking of it, and endeavouring, vainly endeavouring, to arrange what she would say to him.

'Mother,' she said, when Mrs. Bell once went up to her, 'you won't tell Hetta and Phineas, will you: Not today, I mean?' Mrs. Bell agreed that it would be better not to tell them. Perhaps she thought that she had already depended too much on Hetta and Phineas in the matter.

Susan's finery in the way of dress had never been extensive, and now lately, in these last sad winter days, she had thought but little of the fashion of her clothes. But when she began to dress herself for the evening, she did ask her mother with some anxiety what she had better wear. 'If he loves you he will hardly see what you have on,' said the mother. But not the less was she careful to smooth her daughter's hair, and make the most that might be made of those faded roses.

How Susan's heart beat, – how both their hearts beat as the hands of the clock came round to seven! And then, sharp at seven, came the knock; that same short bold ringing knock which Susan had so soon learned to know as belonging to Aaron Dunn. 'Oh mother, I had better go up stairs,' she cried, starting from her chair.

'No dear; you would only be more nervous.'

'I will, mother.'

'No, no dear; you have not time;' and then Aaron Dunn was in the room.

She had thought much what she would say to him, but had not yet quite made up her mind. It mattered however but very little. On whatever she might have resolved, her resolution would have vanished to the wind. Aaron Dunn came into the room, and in one second she found herself in the centre of a whirlwind and his arms were the storms that enveloped her on every side.

'My own, own darling girl,' he said over and over again, as he pressed her to his heart, quite regardless of Mrs. Bell, who stood by, sobbing with joy. 'My own Susan.'

'Aaron, dear Aaron,' she whispered. But she had already recognized the fact that for the present meeting a passive part would become her well, and save her a deal of trouble. She had her lover there quite safe, safe beyond anything that Mr. or Mrs. Beckard might have to say to the contrary. She was quite happy; only that there were symptoms now and again that the whirlwind was about to engulf her yet once more.

'Dear Aaron, I am so glad you are come,' said the innocent-minded widow, as she went up stairs with him, to show him his room; and then he embraced her also. 'Dear, dear mother,' he said.

On the next day there was, as a matter of course, a family conclave. Hetta and Phineas came down, and discussed the whole subject of the coming marriage with Mrs. Bell. Hetta at first was not quite certain; – ought they not to inquire whether the situation was permanent?

'I won't inquire at all,' said Mrs. Bell, with an energy that startled both the daughter and son-in-law. 'I would not part them now; no, not if –' and the widow shuddered as she thought of her daughter's sunken eyes, and pale cheeks.

'He is a good lad,' said Phineas, 'and I trust she will make him a sober steady wife;' and so the matter was settled.

During this time, Susan and Aaron were walking along the Balston road; and they also had settled the matter – quite as satisfactorily.

Such was the courtship of Susan Dunn.

POCKET CLASSICS